Early Praise

This heartwarming story shows the intricate realities of moving on after loss. Bea's prose paints a beautiful image of each emotion and the setting, making the reader feel as if they are present in her story.

Devon Thiele, *author of Burnout*

The book is classic Nicole Bea; the description is lush and the east coast setting is a character in its own right. The world can be impossibly hard, but [Bea] shows us that it can be kind, too.

Zilla Novikov, *author of Query*

Thank You For Loving Me

Nicole Bea

SILVER SHELL PUBLISHING

Thank You For Loving Me

Copyright © 2023 by Nicole Bea

All rights reserved. No part of this publication may be reproduced, stored or transmitted in any form or by any means, electronic, mechanical, photocopying, recording, scanning, or otherwise without written permission from the publisher. It is illegal to copy this book, post it to a website, or distribute it by any other means without permission.

This novel is entirely a work of fiction. The names, characters and incidents portrayed in it are the work of the author's imagination. Any resemblance to actual persons, living or dead, events or localities is entirely coincidental.

Editing by Jennia Herold d'Lima

Contents

Dedication	VII
Content Warning	IX
Chapter One	1
Chapter Two	15
Chapter Three	29
Chapter Four	45
Chapter Five	61
Chapter Six	75
Chapter Seven	91
Chapter Eight	109
Chapter Nine	125
Chapter Ten	145
Chapter Eleven	161
Chapter Twelve	179
Chapter Thirteen	195

Chapter Fourteen	211
Chapter Fifteen	227
Chapter Sixteen	241
Chapter Seventeen	257
Acknowledgments	269
About the Author	271
Also By Nicole Bea	273

To anyone struggling with their grief ship. May you soon find the shore.

Content Warning

Please be advised that this novel includes themes of grief / depression, references to spousal death, and drinking.

Chapter One

I FIND MYSELF WAKING up early most days to work on a painting, even though I don't have to.

The yellow glow coming through my bedroom window matches the paint smeared across my palette and canvas. Fine print that's now faded away on the tube called the shade 'lemon balm' which I hate, because the word 'balm' is too close to 'bomb,' and the thought of anything crashing and burning is too close to my memories of last summer. I call the paint 'egg yolk', which I dislike slightly less. At least eggs are linked to happy memories: the nostalgia of Taylor making me breakfast in bed on the weekends, the hilarious image of his last birthday cake that I tried to bake, the reminder of that time we vacationed at a farm in Charlottetown and were able to pick out our own eggs for brunch. Reminiscing about eggs provides good memories. Thinking about crashing and burning does not.

Breathing a sigh as I stroke my paintbrush over the blank white spaces, I perch a little more comfortably on the edge of the bed. I have a studio at the back of the house, one that overlooks the water and the beach. This morning the blankets feel like a better home for me while I work on this custom piece for a client who commissioned it through my website. Even though there's a dog bed in the studio, Jovi—named after Bon Jovi due to my late husband's love of the artist's music—seems to like being allowed on the comforter more than anything else. He's somewhat patiently waiting for me to say the magic word "walk," and then he'll become sixty pounds of husky fluff hopping up and down until we head toward the ocean's shoreline.

I swish my brush around in the little cup of murky water on the bedside table, looking at the art piece. The sunrise is a bright yellow with tinges of pink and blue, cotton candy colors around the edges of the clouds that hang over the top of the space where I'll add rolling hills and a cottage. So far, the shades are a match to the photo that's laying on the bed next to me. I'm rather proud of myself for color-matching so perfectly despite my distraction this morning. The cerise hue is striking in itself, and I know that recreating it for another painting in exactly the right shade will be impossible. I should charge extra for these perfect colors that I'll never see again. But I don't, and never will. My hand clenches around my paintbrush at the thought, my heart picking up the pace just enough that I feel a difference in the way it beats, while my wedding band—signifying what?—feels tight on my finger.

Jovi lifts his head from the blanket the moment I stop painting, looking at me with his liquid brown eyes. I know he's waiting for that magic word, and he's been so patient with me this morning that I set my brush down on the paint-splattered night table.

"Walk?"

He tilts his head to the side, hesitating for a moment before he launches himself off the end of the bed in a barking flurry of gray fur. He leaves the room and his nails click across the hardwood floor toward the front of the house before I hear him skidding back to the bedroom.

"I'm coming, I'm coming."

I unravel myself from the draw of the bed sheets before setting the wet canvas on the easel in the corner of the room. The wooden stand is situated by the spot where the sunlight is streaking through. Admiring the piece for a moment, I can't help but remember all the sunrises Taylor and I watched from the back patio, our coffees in hand, when he'd come home from duty or would be leaving for work. It takes effort to tear myself away from looking at the colors of the artificial sky—but I remind myself that this isn't my sky. This sky belongs to Cordelia Martin of Saint Peter's, Missouri.

Jovi plops his wet nose in my hand, a reminder that we were going somewhere. I give him a scratch behind the ears as I turn toward the bedroom door, my bare feet sticking to the floor.

"Okay, I'm coming this time, I promise."

The dog takes off like a banshee down the hallway, tail wagging, and I follow behind him with a stifled yawn. The house is illuminated in the same egg yolk color as the bedroom, sparkles of dust floating through the air, nagging at me that I should probably get the vacuum out. It's been a few days and huskies shed more than I anticipated, even though I'd read about their coats online before I made the decision to get Jovi shortly after Taylor died.

Stripping off my painting apron, I hang it on the hook by the front door before reaching for Jovi's leash. It's hard to find the ring on his collar amid his bushy coat and excitement, but I know the moment I hook the lead on and open the door, he'll calm down a little bit.

"Ready for the beach?" He opens his mouth, giving me a dog's smile, and I twist open the doorknob and let the two of us out into the blue and yellow morning.

Eastern Port is small, the rocky beach one of the town's only focal points. It's a destination for those who like the quiet of the coast and want to live on the edge of the ocean without a city's busy nature. Taylor picked Eastern Port because he thought the setting would be a good muse for my paintings and a great place to raise a family. He wasn't wrong. It's quiet and safe and close to good schools. The neighbors seem kind, nodding in my general direction and saying hello when I see them. But my sadness lives here as well, and sometimes that overtakes the gentleness and the compassion of Eastern Port and its people.

Jovi waits for me to close the front door before he tries to race down the front steps, something chattering in the oak tree on one side of the property. I can't see what it is in the tall branches because of the height, and I suspect Jovi can't either, but the sound is enough to put him on alert as we walk down the gravel pathway, through the backyard, and toward the rocky beachfront. I check both ways before crossing the road even though there are rarely any cars here at the end of Marigold Street. Then I break into a quick jog, Jovi following along, running over the short dunes and the seagrass toward the boulders at the edge of the water.

We pick our way over the beach, finding our usual path in between the stormy gray rocks toward the pebbles and sand. Once we get to a safe spot, I unclip his leash and Jovi takes off along the shoreline, no doubt looking for a stick for me to throw into the water. His recall is better than it was only a few months ago, so I've been letting him off-lead on the beach at this end since there's barely ever anyone around for him to bother.

I walk after Jovi, taking my time, the dog leaving shallow pawprints that get washed away by the tide. It's possible to see the house from here, and for a moment I think I see Taylor standing on the back veranda with his coffee mug, watching me and Jovi in the early morning light. It's just a trick of the sun's rays, and I know it, but the mirage makes my heart beat fast and forces me to take a second look, then a third. I blink and shake my head.

He's not there, and he'll never be there again.

My fingers clench around the coiled leash, and even though I'm tired of crying, tears prickle at the corners of my eyes.

Jovi returns to my side with a piece of driftwood clamped between his teeth, the surface a similar off-white to that of a new canvas. I stop walking and he sits patiently at my feet, wiggling a little as a young dog does, before I take the stick from him and toss it out into the calm water. He crashes through the ripples in the water, turning them into splashing waves, doggy-paddling out toward the great blue yonder in order to fetch his prized possession. When he returns to the sand, he drops the driftwood at my feet and I throw it again, over and over, until he finally comes back and doesn't drop the stick.

"You all done?" I ask him as if he's going to respond. He just stares back at me for a moment, eyes wide in puppy introspection, before he lies down on the beach, placing a paw over top of the branch and chewing on the hard end.

I take a seat on the sand next to Jovi, leaning back on my elbows with my face raised up to the sun. It's going to be another scorcher, and I have a list of things to do today, including trying to finish up Cordelia Martin's cottage painting. There's another watercolor waiting in my queue, and I'd prefer not to let my online shop get backed up with custom orders. I like to have time to paint the things I want to, though lately, I've been running low on ideas, stuck browsing through stock art landscapes for inspiration. There's been no way to capture the light properly here in Eastern Port with my phone's camera. I'm not a great photographer anyway.

Out toward the harbor, a frigate cruises along the varying shades of blue. The steely gray of the ship is a contrast in colors, though it only appears as a dot in the distance. Seeing the vessel reminds me of Taylor's dream to be in the Navy—a dream I encouraged him to follow, and a dream his family didn't approve of. His sister Caitlyn especially hated it because it eventually meant Taylor was away on deployment during their father's passing from pancreatic cancer. Caitlyn said that was my fault as well; my fault for pushing Taylor. My fault he took the posting in Eastern Port.

Shaking my head, I squint out toward the crystalline ocean. There's not much to see but the city in the distance and then the flatness of whatever else lies beyond. For a little while, I'm in the moment, Jovi's teeth cracking on the driftwood stick amid the lapping of the foaming water. I dig the toes of my shoes in the sand, thinking about how fast a year can go by, but also how slow and painful every day can feel.

The therapist provided by the military resource center assured me that I'd move on from the shipwreck that killed Taylor. She said I'd never forget him, but the days would become easier. She also made every explanation into a military analogy, which didn't always work for me, until she compared my sadness and loss to the sea.

"Grief is like a wave," she noted, scribbling notes down on her pad of lined yellow paper. She let the thought sit with me for a moment before continuing. "The waves overcome your ship, and you feel like you're drowning, gasping, begging for a lifeboat to come save you. But then, eventually, the waves no longer capsize the boat. They rock it, they splash over the edges, but you're no longer at risk of drowning."

She looked up at me, setting her pen down on the pad. "You hang on to a piece of something, a memory, an object, an idea, and when that wave comes, that's the thing that keeps you afloat. Then, one day, the waves aren't fifty feet tall anymore. They're bumps in a safe harbor. They're ripples on the beach. They never stop, never disappear entirely, but you can take your boat through them. You can sail your ship. And you can get ready for your next big adventure."

I hated the comparison. Losing Taylor was nothing like the sea, except maybe for the feeling of drowning. The sensation that every breath I took was dragging me closer to the ocean floor. The notion that I'd find a way through the loss and guilt and grief and pain of losing him seemed impossible. Caitlyn didn't so much as blame me, not verbally, but her expression said something along the lines of "you pushed him into this stupid dream, and now he's dead."

I sigh, sitting up and wiping my sand-covered palms on my shorts. Jovi looks at me expectantly, as if he's hoping we're going to play fetch again, but I'm on a mission to finish Cordelia Martin's painting before supper. Eyeing the ship again in the distance, I give the boat a subtle nod—my version of those folks who cross their hearts while saying the name of the Father, Son, and Holy Spirit—before rising to my feet and calling Jovi to my side. He brings his driftwood along; another piece to add to the pile in the backyard.

We walk down the beach slower than we did when we arrived, the sun beating down on us in a mid-morning heatwave. Sand squishes beneath my feet as Jovi and I make our way to the boulders, and just as we're hopping up to the dunes, a man comes over the seagrass-coated hill with a large German shepherd in tow.

Most people in this town aren't familiar to me. Taylor and I hadn't lived here long before the accident, and since then, I haven't ventured out much. Past the beach, StopShop Grocery Mart, and occasionally A Cup or Two for an iced cappuccino, I basically live in the studio in the back of the house. However, something— the smoothness of his shirt, the lack of sand on his shoes—says that this man isn't from here.

"Here, Jovi. Wait." I reach down for his collar and snap on the leash as the man comes up the dune path, a camera bag strapped over his shoulder and the German shepherd's leash wound around his wrist.

The dog is beautiful, but the thing that strikes me immediately as the two approach and then pass is the color of the man's eyes peeking out from under his ball cap: pale blue and clear like the Caribbean. I swear the sound of the surf and the depths of the water echo through them in the split second I notice their shade, filling me with a sudden, sinking feeling; a reminder of my loss. The man nods a hello, giving me a polite half-smile, before passing with his dog and heading down to the ocean's edge.

A moment passes before I smile back, but he's already gone, and I've already had my imaginary boat smash into a wave I wasn't expecting. But as the resource therapist said, that's the other thing about grief. It can hit you when you don't expect it.

Walking back up the grassy knoll toward the house, I mix theoretical paints in my head to try to create the color blue of that man's eyes as a distraction from thinking about

Taylor. None of my tubes of acrylics or pots of watercolors are quite right. Maybe this is another instance where there's a perfect color out there in the world that I'll never be able to recreate.

Jovi drops his stick on the porch with a *thunk*, and it startles me back to real life. My brain has been all over the place today, and it's still early. I'll make some tea to help me focus, crawl back on the bed, and try to get some more of the cottage painting finished. After that, I'll vacuum and tidy. I know the last part is a lie—I'll be up half the night finishing this piece—but if I tell myself I'm going to do it then at least I can say I had good intentions.

My fingers are on the doorknob when my cell phone rings from inside the house, and a sense of dread falls over me. There's only one person who calls me other than telemarketers and occasionally the bank, and that's Caitlyn. I'm in no rush to talk to her, just as I'm sure she has no great desire to talk to me. But this Friday is the one-year anniversary of Taylor's death, and she's probably calling to get the conversation out of the way so that on the actual day of his passing she can, I don't know, sit in her own home and remind herself that everything's my fault.

Jovi walks in ahead of me, and I take my time unhooking his lead, the phone's jingle playing in the background. By the time I've kicked off my shoes by the door and let him past me in the entryway, the call has ended, and there's a little *bloop bloop* signifying that I have a new voicemail.

Picking up the phone off the counter, I poke at the home button and '1 Missed Call' pops up, showing me Caitlyn's name. Just as I expected.

With a sigh—I seem to be doing a lot of that today—I punch the voicemail button and then hit the speaker option.

"Hello, Maggie. I hope you're well. Thought I'd check in, but you must be out with the dog."

There's a lengthy pause. Maybe Caitlyn's using the space in the one-sided conversation to try and remember Jovi's name, though she always calls him "the dog" even if I've just reminded her. I look down at the phone screen but the call time counter is still going, meaning Caitlyn's message isn't over yet.

"Anyway, I'm sure you remember that Friday's the anniversary of Taylor's... Taylor. I'll call you back then. You don't have to call me."

The call goes silent then. Caitlyn hung up without even bothering to say goodbye, which isn't totally unlike her. She prefers to leave things short and to the point. As the screen brightens back to displaying recent calls, I click the trash can icon and delete Caitlyn's message. She'll call again on Friday, so I don't need to remember to return her call.

I set the phone on the kitchen counter, and look down to where Jovi's sitting, patiently waiting for his breakfast. Flicking on the kettle that's already a quarter filled with water from last night, I open a plastic bin and reach in for the dry food scoop before pouring the cup into his bowl. Jovi wiggles a little bit, wagging his tail and shifting from foot to foot, impatient for his meal, but he knows to wait now. When he was smaller, not so much.

The electric kettle makes a little bubbling noise in the background.

"Good boy, Jovi. Okay."

He trots toward his dish, collar tags jingling against the stainless steel as he munches away. Meanwhile, I reach up into the cupboard for a mug, looking for the pink watercolor one I painted back in university at Cottage Crafts. It's almost the same cerise in my memory as the paint I mixed this morning, and maybe that's why I'm looking for it today. However, the cupboard is packed with too many mugs, and as I shift one, it hits another, one tips, and three come falling off the shelf. I manage to catch two of them, but the third smashes on the floor, sending Jovi skittering away just long enough for me to see which cup has broken.

The mug was one of Taylor's favorites: an egg yolk yellow with "you're egg-cellent" written on one side. Now, the physical reminder I didn't even know I had has exploded into splintered pieces all over the kitchen's tile floor.

Maybe I can't associate eggs with happy memories anymore. Maybe every egg is a shipwreck waiting to happen. Maybe every bit of yellow is a painful reminder.

Instead of picking up the mug's pieces, I slide my back along the bottom cupboard and sit down amid the destruction. Tears prickle the corners of my eyes, the waves approaching my theoretical boat, lashing at the sides and causing the vessel to tip. If I cry, I'll never get Cordelia Martin's painting done today. If I cry, I will capsize. If I cry...

Jovi walks around the kitchen island, away from the broken ceramic pieces, and lays down with his head on my lap. Absently, I pet his gray and white fur and stare at the living room wall. It's painted the same egg yolk yellow as the mug, as the lemon balm paint, and as the sunrise, and suddenly I hate it. Because egg yolks smash and lemon balm is too close to "bomb" and the sunrise reminds me of Taylor's weekend breakfasts in bed. Breakfasts I'll never have again.

Chapter Two

An hour and a half later, splattered droplets of a color called "sea breeze" pepper the living room's hardwood floor. I didn't think to pick up a drop cloth when I was at House 'N Home buying supplies and therefore the paint I'm rolling over the yellow accent wall not only covers the space I'm trying to paint, but also my clothes and hands. Even if I don't do the best job in the world, I'll feel better with a new color on the wall. Something not the same shade as Taylor's memory.

I know I should be working on Cordelia Martin's cottage painting, but I'm certain that I won't be able to focus on it knowing this wall's color needs to be changed. It's making me feel a little better, slapping this sea breeze blue paint over the yellow. I might not feel as pleased later when I have to clean paint off the floor.

Thinking of cleaning, it strikes me that I didn't even bother sweeping up the broken mug before I left for House 'N Home. The puzzle of exploded pieces sits on my mind as I touch up the side of the wall where I accidentally used a dollop of too much paint. I almost don't want to touch the ceramic shards, not because I'm afraid of cutting my fingers on them or because throwing them out will mean getting rid of another piece of Taylor, but because it's not a priority. The priority right now is rage painting this wall until the lemon-balm-bomb-egg-yolk yellow disappears into the void and stops eating away at me.

Jovi lays curled up on the worn beige couch that sits out in the middle of the floor so I can paint behind it, the fabric looking a little sad. It's times like this one when I'm able to see the age of the furniture—the back looking much newer and much less faded than the front. Jovi doesn't seem to care though, and neither do I in the end because everything's covered in a fine coating of dog hair as it is, and nobody ever comes to visit anyway.

I slather more paint on the roller from the plastic tray and reach up as high as I can to meet the spot where I've already cut the blue onto the line of the ceiling with green painter's tape. The contrast between the two colors is rather ugly, but at least it's temporary until "sea breeze" dries and I can pull off the long strips of tape edging the accent wall. Thankfully, I thought to buy paint with primer already mixed in, so I don't have to repeat this process. A little more expensive, but for someone who hates painting on anything but a canvas, it was worth the extra money.

After a couple more swipes of the roller, the yellow completely disappears, and I don't think twice about leaving the color behind. Placing the painting tools in the tray on the floor, I walk backward across the room to admire my work. The strokes from the roller are still visible in the wet paint and the late afternoon sunlight, but the color is pretty and beachy which is a perfect fit for the beachfront location. While the yellow was sunny and bright, "sea breeze" offers a bit more dimension to the room's open concept design, joined with the kitchen and dining area.

"What do you think, Jovi?" I ask, looking down at the dozing dog who just barely opens his eyes in response to hearing his name. "Do you like the color?"

Jovi lifts his head for a moment, looking toward the front door in case I've suddenly decided to take him back to the beach. A few seconds later, when I don't move toward the door, he puts his head back down.

"Well, I like it. I think it's a nice change." I'm not saying the words to anyone in particular, not even Jovi, because I'm trying to convince myself that the change is good and that I didn't just cover up something I didn't really want to lose.

That thought makes me choke up a little, and I cough to try and make the sensation go away. Unfortunately, it doesn't seem to do anything other than make me have to cough a second time, now a bit louder.

With a lump in my throat, I pick up the painting supplies and bring them into the kitchen, careful to step around the broken mug pieces. Running hot water over the cheap materials to try and clean them as best as possible, I let everything soak with peony-scented dish soap. I fetch a broom from the pantry and finally sweep up the yellow and white ceramic bits into the dustpan before dumping them into the garbage can under the sink. They clink together as they fall, tinkling like scattered music. I stare at the open bin for a moment and the little pieces of other garbage around

Taylor's mug, and I choke back tears knowing that they're all going to the landfill. The wrappers, the "egg-cellent" mug, my memories. Everything is in the trash.

I let go of the lid a little harder than necessary, and it slams shut hard enough that it startles Jovi from where he's sitting across the room.

"Sorry, sorry..." I murmur before placing the broom and pan back in the pantry much more quietly and closing the door.

Jovi hops down from the couch cushions amid my noise and comes into the kitchen area for a drink of water from his bowl. I watch as he slurps and flicks droplets around on the mat with his messy tongue, tail slowly wagging. When he's done, water dribbling from his muzzle, I give him a soft smile.

"Want to go finish the painting in the bedroom?" Jovi tilts his head to the side at the question, and I know that he knows the word bedroom means he gets to be on the bed. "Come on, let's go to bed."

Jovi trots off down the hallway to the bedroom, disappearing through the doorway. I follow suit, shoving my phone in my pocket in case Caitlyn happens to call back, my bare feet sticking to the hardwood. Cordelia Martin's painting sits in the corner between rays of afternoon sunshine, the ideal cerise sunrise looking even more perfect in this lighting. I find myself experiencing a wave of pride in my work that I don't often feel since Taylor passed. He was always my painting cheerleader, even if he did think it was more of a hobby. Without him, I've had to become my own cheering section, and it doesn't work as well.

By the time I lift Cordelia Martin's painting from the easel, Jovi's made himself comfortable in his previous spot on the blankets, my tubes of paint still scattered around where I was sitting this morning. It takes a few minutes to organize myself on the bed— plumping up pillows to support my back against the headboard, swishing brushes around through the gray water in the cup on the nightstand. Finally, I crawl across the mattress and make a little nest of sheets, sitting cross-legged on top of the white fabric. Jovi snores and I mix paints to make the perfect shade to match the log cabin in the picture.

I'm just about to swipe a dab of woodsy brown on the canvas when I hear Taylor's voice saying my name. It sounds far away, like it's coming over faded radio waves or from underwater, but it's there. I hear it.

Everything stops.

"Maggie."

There it is again, and my paintbrush—complete with a daub of brown paint—falls right across the perfect pink sunrise I'd worked so hard on this morning. But it doesn't matter because I swear I just heard Taylor calling for me, speaking my name, even though it was distant, like he's here somewhere in this room. My heart pounds, beating like an erratic drum behind my ribs—I know I heard him say it, say Maggie, the name coming from his mouth somewhere in the deep yonder of the house.

I strain my ears to hear it again, the rumble of words across dimensions getting lost in the creaks of the house and the brilliance of the dusty sunshine. There's a constant hum of his voice, as if it's trying to get through, but no words are clear enough to make out except for my name.

Maggie.

Very slowly, I set the canvas down on the blankets, the brush rolling off and making a mahogany mark across the painting and the white sheets. I don't care because I still hear the hum, the panic of hearing Taylor's voice is still in my chest, and my fingers are shaking so hard I can barely lift myself from the bed. But when I do, the hum grows louder. There are more words.

"Late... you... love."

The voice is coming from behind me and I spin on my heel so fast I clatter into the easel, startling Jovi awake again. But this time I don't apologize to him because I very nearly expect Taylor to be standing in the bedroom doorway, his brown eyes watching me with amusement. The banging in my chest gets harder, faster, almost painful with how much I desperately want to see him, but when I focus on the space between me and the hallway wall, there's nobody there.

Instead, from the back pocket of my shorts comes my phone, crashing to the floor and scaring me so much that I let out a little scream.

From the device is the murmuring hum of Taylor's voice: "I'll see you at supper. Love you, Mags." Then a click where the sound dissolves into nothing except the haunting emptiness of a space he'll never be in again, in a house that might never be a home without him.

The room is quiet, the silence echoing in my ears like the crash and clatter of my whirlwind. As I bend down to reach for the device, it lights up to show my Messages screen. It strikes me that I must have accidentally dialed my voicemail box when I sat with the phone on the bed, playing through all of Taylor's old messages saved from over a year ago.

I stand and flick out of the app before taking a seat down on the edge of the bed, my rapidly beating heart making me feel on edge and shaky. Maybe I need to talk to someone. Maybe I need to get out of this stifling house. Maybe all the paint fumes are getting to me. While I'm considering all of the above, Jovi scoots across the bed and places his head on my lap, like he always does when he wants to be petted or when he thinks something might be wrong.

I don't know exactly how long I sit there, but after some time goes by, my heartbeat slows and I'm able to process some tiny semblance of logical thoughts. Staring at the device, my fingers vibrating, I punch the name of one of the only contacts left in my phone, returning the call from earlier that I was told I didn't need to return.

Caitlyn answers after what feels like the fiftieth ring. "Hi, Maggie. I said you didn't have to call me back." Her voice is flat, as usual, as it always is when we talk to each other out of obligation rather than any actual desire.

I open my mouth to speak, but nothing comes out. Just a croak from my throat, and I realize that I don't know what I planned on saying to her because she certainly won't want to hear that I thought I heard Taylor talking to me. "Um, hi. I know. I just…"

I just what? Thought I'd call back anyway? Wanted to talk to another human being? Might be losing my mind?

Caitlyn sounds confused when she speaks. "Are you okay?"

The question is meant to be something I say yes to and for Caitlyn and I to move on from, but for whatever reason—for *every* reason—I can't lie to her today. She might not really care that I'm not okay, but she's at least someone who will listen, right?

I suck in a deep breath, running my fingers not holding the phone over Jovi's head.

"I… I thought I heard Taylor talking to me. I heard his voice saying my name while I was working on a commission, but it was just my voicemail playing. And this morning I thought I saw him on the patio while I was at the beach. I know he's gone, Caitlyn, but what if my brain isn't accepting it? What if I'm never going to accept it? What if he's trying to tell me something and these are just messages from wherever his spirit is?"

Once my mouth opens, I can't stop. I talk at Caitlyn for a solid ten minutes about both scenarios, speaking so fast that by the time I give her an opportunity to reply, I'm out of breath and coughing again, half on the verge of vomiting. Even though I hold my hand over the phone and away from my mouth as I bend over and hack between my knees on the side of the mattress, I'm sure Caitlyn's wondering if she can just hang up on me until I get a grip or puke my guts out or both.

Once I catch my breath, slowing my coughing and getting my choking down to intermittent, awkward sobs, Caitlyn replies.

"Maggie, he's gone. We both know he's gone. People don't send messages from the dead, and they certainly don't call and make you listen to old voicemails." Her voice is serious as usual, but there's a tiny touch of softness around the edges as if she might be feeling something too. As if the impending anniversary of Taylor's passing might be making her feel... anything.

"I know, I mean, I think I know."

"You do know, Maggie. Maybe you need to go back to the resource center and see if they're able to do anything more for you. I'm not a therapist. I don't have anything to tell you other than what you already know."

I can't tell if she means what I already know like this whole thing being my fault, or if I know that Taylor isn't coming back. Either way, I'm acutely aware of both, and I'm not able to do anything about either one. And really, I don't know what I expected Caitlyn to do other than listen. She used to be such a good listener—back before Taylor passed, back when we were in high school and I fell in and out of relationships with others before Taylor and I finally admitted our mutual affections.

I remember sitting on Caitlyn's bed crying over some boy whose name I can't even remember now, and she handed me a glass of water and a miniature candy bar from somewhere in her regular hiding place for sweets: the top dresser drawer.

"You should only care about boys who smudge your lipstick, not your mascara," she said. It took me a moment to understand what exactly she was referring to, but when my brain finally locked in on her reference, it made me smile.

Those were the days when Caitlyn and I were friends. The days before all of these dark ones fell in on us and changed the dynamic of our relationship.

I creep back into the present day, realizing that I haven't said anything in a few moments because I was stuck in past memories.

"I… that's not the point. I just, I wanted to get my thoughts out."

There's a sigh on the other end of the line, and I picture Caitlyn twirling a strand of her curly hair around her finger like she would have with one of the old phone cords when we were kids. "Don't you have friends you can call? Anyone in that town you can meet up with for dinner or something? Surely after a year and a half you must know people to get out of the house with. It's not healthy staying inside and talking to that dog all the time."

I'm positive she knows I don't have anyone but her—and I suspect the question is designed to dig the theoretical knife in a little bit farther. "I don't really know anyone here, no.

People are nice but they're not the same, you know? I'm still a stranger to them."

"Have you tried to meet anyone, Maggie?"

The questions sting, right behind my eyes where they start to water with salty tears. Meet anyone? I've never needed anyone but Taylor, especially after Mom passed away. I didn't have siblings—I was often on my own anyway. I like my own company. But admittedly, I'm lonely now, even with Jovi.

"I..." There's hesitation in my voice and I can't help but feel like I'm being chastised for something I didn't phone about in the first place. Maybe I shouldn't have bothered returning Caitlyn's call. Maybe I shouldn't return them ever again. "I painted one of the walls in the house. It was too yellow."

There's silence on the other end of the line for at least a solid thirty seconds as I try to guess what's going on in Caitlyn's head. She's probably trying to decipher what the point of talking to me even is, or why we still keep in contact when the person we both loved is gone. Meanwhile, I'm over here in Eastern Port in a paint-fume-filled house, sweating in the summer heat, waiting for my estranged sister-in-law to tell me... I don't even know what.

"He did love the color yellow," Caitlyn replies slowly, her voice warbling a little as she lets out another sigh. "Why'd you paint over it?"

"I broke his mug."

"You painted a wall because you broke Taylor's mug?"

I nod, even though Caitlyn can't see the movement, and Jovi curls around next to my thigh. "It was yellow too."

"Ah." She breathes out the word as if it all makes perfect sense, and that my rationale for completing a small home renovation isn't completely and totally ridiculous. "What color is it now?"

I flop back on the bed, barely careful enough to avoid the painting and palette that I've left on the sheets. "It's called sea breeze. Clear blue, like the ocean. Well, the ocean you see in pictures from vacations down south."

"Must look nice."

"Yeah. Something different."

Another pause in the conversation; I watch the ceiling fan twirl around and around without being acutely aware of how much time passes. Finally, Caitlyn coughs and clears her throat to disperse some of the one-sided awkward quiet she seems to be experiencing. For me, hearing her breathe on the other end of the phone provides some inherent comfort.

"I've got to go, Maggie. But I'll talk to you Friday."

I barely shift my position from lying on the bed watching the blades of the fan when I reply. "Sounds good."

A follow-up emptiness exists in the moment where neither of us knows if it's appropriate to say goodbye. Another quiet Caitlyn works to fill as quickly as possible before it becomes unbearable for her. "Try not to... just—have a good rest of your day."

"You too." I lift the phone from my ear and go to press the red "call end" button, but before I tap it, it disappears, signifying Caitlyn ended the conversation before I had a chance.

I stay there on the bed, watching the fan jiggle gently, until Jovi wakes up from beside me and hops off the bed to stretch. It's then that I remember Cordelia Martin's painting with the big streak through it that's now most definitely dry. Heaving myself up, I collect my paints and the canvas, looking over the brown splatter to see what I can do to fix it. The cerise color I loved so much is ruined. I'll have to mix up some more but it will never be as pretty as it was the first time.

Cordelia Martin will never know that her pink sky used to be more beautiful. But I'll know. And I'll have to live with it, just like I'll have to live with the knowledge that underneath the sea breeze blue paint in the living room is a whole wall of Taylor yellow.

Chapter Three

Thanks to my mishap with the mahogany paint, along with the demise of the perfect pink sky, I don't finish Cordelia Martin's canvas until Thursday afternoon. I just barely make it to the postal outlet before they close for the day, squeaking in as the clerk is about to leave. I get the painting into a bubble mailer and seal it shut, fill out all the necessary paperwork, and escape the heat of the shop in only a few minutes. It must be record time for the transaction because I swear every other time I've sent a commission, it takes at least fifteen minutes to get my receipt with the tracking number.

I greet Jovi at home before sticking the long slip of paper on the fridge under a magnet shaped like a cartoon rainbow. I'll probably end up checking the tracking every day until the painting arrives in Missouri just to make sure it arrives safely.

Back in the studio, I fire up my laptop and send a quick email to Cordelia Martin to let her know her painting has shipped before marking it off in the queue and opening up the photo details for my next commission. Someone named Wilhelmina Dare has requested a small piece, the indicated canvas size barely bigger than my hand, of a pretty beach sky in orange and red watercolors. I've completed something similar before, and my memory seems to recall the other had a moon at the top where this one has a flock of birds. Either way, there are similarities that I can draw on, and I spend the night with Jovi in the room at the back of the house, listening to old ballads and painting with my multicolored palettes on the special watercolor canvas.

I lose myself in the moment and stay up much too late to get the piece for Wilhelmina Dare almost completely finished. By the time I realize it's long past dark, Jovi's asleep in his circular dog bed on the floor by my feet, and my hands are covered in shades of pink and tangerine. Plopping the brush in one of the many cups of grayish water around the studio, I stand back and look at the piece. The glimmer of light off the water looks just right, and the touches of white that need to be added once everything is dry will complete the four-inch piece.

Wondering for a moment where Wilhelmina Dare is going to display such a tiny commission, I absently pick little dried globs of "sea breeze" out from underneath my short fingernails. No matter how hard I scrub or how much soap I use, I always seem to have a layer of paint on my hands, and yesterday's purchase of Paint and Prime was thicker and more permanent than what I'd normally use for my artwork so it's harder to wash off.

As Jovi sighs in his sleep, I swap my gaze from the painting down to my phone sitting on the studio table next to his bed. Poking at the black screen, a brilliant glow emits from the device and lights up the space. 12:04 a.m. It's Friday.

It's officially been one year since Taylor died.

For some reason, I almost expect the phone to ring as I'm looking at it, Caitlyn on the other end, ready to say something flat and unfeeling. But, of course, no reasonable person would call in the middle of the night on an anniversary like this one. It's not like it's New Year's Eve or a milestone birthday. It's a memorial. A forget-me-not. A countdown to the next year, and the next, and the one after that.

I thought I'd feel something different, some crashing, capsizing wave of emotion, but I feel nothing like that. I'm tired, I'm proud of my painting, and I have a touch of a headache. I also have a whole lot of a desire to put on my pajamas and crawl under the bedsheets with the ceiling fan blowing down on my face. But as for feelings about Taylor, nothing has magically changed. I'm not over him, but the ship is still upright, ripples rocking the theoretical boat a little bit to and fro. It's strange. I expected... more.

"Jovi, come on. It's bedtime." I stop picking at my fingers long enough to untie my apron, placing it on the table before flicking off the light and heading down the hallway. Jovi follows behind me, nails click-click-clicking, the corridor lit by a nightlight plugged into a socket. Jovi watches as I brush my teeth and wash the paint splatters from my skin as much as possible. Then he crawls on the bed to wait for me to change into my soft pajama pants.

Moonlight glows through the window, and Jovi crawls up into the empty space on the queen-sized bed and rests his head on the other pillow, in almost the same way a person would. It's been a funny quirk of his ever since I brought him home. It feels almost like he's trying to take up space for my comfort, just like how Caitlyn tries to fill in the gaps in our awkward telephone conversations for her own convenience.

With the bedroom bathed in ivory and midnight blue, I pull the thin sheet up over my body and curl next to Jovi. We are engulfed in the ticking sound of the spinning overhead fan, and soon I find myself drifting off to sleep. My dreams are filled with the colors in Wilhelmina Dare's painting, melted orange and raspberry glow, walking on the beach with Jovi and the blue-eyed man who inspired the change to my living room, and, most randomly, the woman—Josie?—from House 'N Home who helped me pick out "sea breeze" and mixed the paint in the shaker machine.

Taylor doesn't appear at all, which feels odd because he's the only thing on my mind.

When I wake up, I bring tea, buttered toast, and a yawning Jovi into the silent, sunny studio where I perch in the reading nook on worn, plaid cushions. House 'N Home had some nice pillows on sale when I was there, and I decide I should drop by this morning and pick them up to freshen the studio space a little bit. Crunching on my toast, I consider what the best color might be in the pale green room—maybe a chocolate brown or an ivory. Better than this old red, white, and black pattern.

As thoughts are rolling around in my head, Jovi patiently sitting at my side and waiting for a crust, I stare out into the yard and across the street to the ocean. Today would be another good day to take Jovi for a walk on the beach, the sun peeking over the dunes down the hill and offering a lemony sunrise with cerulean tinges and tendrils. There aren't any clouds to be seen except one tiny puff high up in the sky, curled like cotton batting and stretched lengthwise. Maybe if I take Jovi out now, I'll miss an early morning call from Caitlyn, reminding me with the tone of her voice once again that this is all my fault.

I'm just taking a final bite of toast when I realize I haven't tasted any of it, my mind already overwhelmed, and it's only eight in the morning. It's not going to be a good day to make decisions. I hope there aren't too many cushion options at House 'N Home. Rising from my spot by the window, Jovi looks at me expectantly; I feed him the top crust from the bread and he swallows it in one mouthful.

"What do you want to do today?" I ask him, heading down the corridor. In the open concept kitchen-slash-living room, the new blue wall greets me in an ocean-colored morning radiance. "Want to come pick out pillows? Want to go to the store?"

I can't say the word "beach" because Jovi'll start barking and running around the house, and I'd like a chance to get ready. However, I flick my gaze out the kitchen window over the sink and think. It only takes a second, but I'm surprised when Jovi lets out a bark as if he's reading my mind or can see the ocean out the high-up glass panes himself.

"We aren't going yet, Jovi. Do you want your breakfast?"

For a moment, it seems as if he understands my response. But then, as I open the plastic container of dog food and fill up the measuring cup, he lets out another bark and leaves my side to trot toward the front door. Clearly whatever is going on there is much more interesting than food, and with a furrowed brow I walk to the entryway to see what Jovi's so curious about.

I'm halfway across the living room when there's a sturdy knock at the door.

My first reaction is to freeze and pretend I'm not home or not awake or maybe in the bathroom showering, while my second reaction is to look over at the mirror conveniently hanging on the closet door and realize that I look like I just fell out of bed. Which I did. So, my disheveled reflection is not entirely unexpected, but I might scare whoever is at the door.

As quickly as I can, I stand in the middle of the room and pull my hair up into a smoother ponytail. There isn't enough time to run and change into something else, so I'll have to hope it's just kids selling cookies, raising money for an after-school activity. They won't care what I look like so long as I buy something.

I cross the room, getting whacked in the leg by Jovi's wagging tail as I put my hand on the doorknob. The rare times we have someone come to the house, he gets excited.

"Sit, Jovi. Wait."

Jovi slowly slinks down onto his bum, tail thumping against the hardwood floor in time with the second, louder, knock at the door.

Grabbing the knob, I open the door, expecting a bunch of children in soccer jerseys or Girl Guide outfits, but instead it's the blue-eyed man from the beach and his German shepherd, who sits patiently at his side. I give him the fastest once-over that I think I've ever given a man: he's dressed in the type of naval uniform I most often saw Taylor in, primarily black with rank badges and his surname in a matching patch—SMITH, it reads, instead of MONTGOMERY, as Taylor's did. His beard is trimmed short, along with his blond hair, and his shoulder muscles press against the fit of his shirt. Not that I'm looking in an appreciative way, it's more of an observation in comparison to my noodle arms and paint-stained hands.

"Hi, um, I think you probably have the wrong house?" I stammer out like I haven't talked to another human being since Taylor died. Which, in some ways, I haven't. I haven't spoken to anyone in the Navy except for his old captain when he offered his condolences and the woman in the resource department for guidance and grief management.

The man at the door, Smith, gives me a gentle smile, showing a small gap between his two front teeth along with a deep dimple. He shakes his head. "Maggie Montgomery, right? Taylor's..." He trails off, probably not sure what to call me. Taylor's wife? Taylor's widow? Taylor's *something*, that's for sure.

I'm just about to say yes, I am indeed Maggie Montgomery, but before I have a chance to even open my mouth, Jovi takes off out the front door and down the steps, barking his fool head off at the shepherd. The shepherd, meanwhile, stands and turns toward Jovi with its mouth hanging open, tightening the slack in the lead. Jovi bounces up and down the staircase toward the dog and Mr. Smith, wanting desperately to play.

"Jovi! Come!" I call his name with a sharpness to my voice so he knows I'm serious, but instead of slinking into the house, Jovi takes off through the yard barking and running back and forth like this new dog is the most exciting dog he's ever seen in his life. Little blades of emerald green grass fling up and down in the air from underneath his paws and I repeat my command, now a little bit firmer. "Come!"

Mr. Smith grins, holding the shepherd's leash toward me. "I'll go grab him so you don't have to go outside in your pajamas. This is Perdita." He looks down at her. "Sit." She immediately does as she's told, unlike my dog who is running around the yard as if he's never been trained to do anything except act like a wired puppy.

I stand there in the doorway with this strange man's dog, watching him walk down the stairs and out onto the grass that badly needs to be mowed. He leans over and picks up a tennis ball that he's found God knows where, and tosses it toward Jovi's general direction so it lands near his feet. Distracted, Jovi does a sideways leap nearly right into Mr. Smith, grabbing for the ball just as the man kneels down and takes hold of the collar that's almost completely hidden underneath Jovi's gray and white scruff. Knowing he's been caught, Jovi settles immediately, and Mr. Smith brings him up the steps and onto the patio with his blue eyes sparkling in what I can only presume is amusement.

Ushering Jovi into the house and handing over Perdita's lead, careful not to touch hands with the man, I clear my throat. "So, what can I help you with, Mr. Smith?"

"Please, call me Grayson." His voice is deep and rocky, and there's a little twinge in my stomach at the sound of his name that I force myself to push away because I don't know what it means.

"Grayson. Perfect. Thanks for catching Jovi." I nod back toward the inside of the house which I'm now blocking, Jovi's nose just sticking out from behind my leg to sniff at Perdita. "We don't usually have visitors this early in the morning."

Grayson clears his throat, his expression turning a bit more serious. "I'm sorry for the early hour. I'm still on ship's time. It's just that I have something that belongs to you. Well, something that should belong to you. From Taylor."

I narrow my eyes, tilting my head a little to the side. This has to be some kind of sick joke. Someone coming here on the anniversary of Taylor's death, some stranger, to tell me that he has something from my husband?

"What do you mean, you have something from Taylor? You... you do know he died a year ago?" The word "died" sticks in my throat like I'm trying to swallow a wad of gum.

Grayson nods, a pained look crossing his face for a split second. "I know. We worked alongside one another for a while."

"Oh, I'm sorry. I guess I just..."

"You don't need to apologize, Maggie. I knew this would probably be painful, but I thought it would be in your best interests to have this, and I figured if I waited too long, I'd run out of courage to come up here and give it to you without knowing what's written inside."

He pulls a small, white envelope from the pocket of his dark slacks and passes it over to me, sealed side up. I hesitate to touch it at first because there's something strange about this, and part of me wonders whether I touch this bit of paper if I'll suddenly hear laughing and it will all be a prank. But I take the envelope between my fingers and flip it over, and, sure enough, Taylor's distinctive blockish handwriting is on the other side.

MAGGIE

Seeing the little curl to the letter 'E' that Taylor always added makes me very nearly break on the outside as hard as I'm struggling on the inside. There's a knot at the base of my throat, threatening to spill up, over, and out of my mouth all over this Grayson's shoes. But I don't want him to know that. He's a stranger, and I'd rather have a breakdown inside with Jovi than in public at my front door.

However, there's something about the delicate company he is providing—whether he knows that he's providing it or not—that almost makes me not want him to leave.

I bite the inside of my cheek so hard I think that I pick up the metallic taste of blood, but if I do, it's only a drop and nothing more. Nothing like the rushing of blood through my heart as I stand here with my arm outstretched and this letter in between my fingers like it's going to kill me if I open it or if it comes too close to my body. My mind races with what it could possibly say, and though I assume it's a note or a small card, the words are a mystery. Taylor wasn't much for sentimental notions and gestures; Valentine's Day and our anniversary were exceptions. And weekends, in a way. Those breakfasts showed he cared more than bringing me flowers ever could.

Grayson coughs, and it's then that I realize I've been standing here awkwardly for at least a minute without saying anything. "I'll let you get back to your day. I hope whatever's inside brings you some comfort."

Before I know what I'm doing, I reply, "Wait."

He looks over at me with his blue eyes, the ones I remember so vividly, while Jovi pushes his full weight against my leg in a second attempt to escape. "Is everything okay?"

The question is loaded, explosive, but I don't think Grayson knows just how not okay things are. Maybe he doesn't know today is the anniversary of Taylor's death. He said he worked with him but that doesn't mean he knows everything about him.

Biting his bottom lip as if he's heard my thoughts, Grayson corrects himself. "Sorry, I know that everything can't be okay. Not after getting something like this a year later."

"Exactly a year later."

"Yeah, I know."

I don't ask him how he knows, or how he remembers, because right now it doesn't matter. What matters is the way I feel, numb but scared and curious and overwhelmed.

We stand there in silence again, and I toy with the envelope, grazing my fingers along the bold letters spelling out "MAGGIE." I can almost feel the indentation where the pen pressed on the paper, and I can't help but imagine Taylor sitting at a desk somewhere writing.

"Did you want to be alone while you open that?" Grayson reaches down to touch his shepherd's head, as if he's just as nervous about standing here on my patio as I am about being by myself while I read what's inside.

"Honestly?" I breathe in some of the warm morning air, allowing it to fill my lungs as Jovi finally stops pressing against me and gives up his demand to go back into the yard. "I don't know."

Grayson's formal stance drops just a little. "I'm so sorry."

There isn't a good response when someone tells you that they're sorry the love of your life has died. I've found that not saying anything at all most frequently works best, because "I'm sorry" is one of those statements that doesn't need a response. They're not meant to be replied to. They're meant to make the other person feel better, not the person experiencing the loss. But something chews on my insides just a little, just enough to notice, telling me that Grayson's experienced a loss as well, even if he only worked with him for a short time. That maybe his grief boat is still out on the waves somewhere, whereas mine is in rippled water.

So this time, I reply. "I'm sorry too."

Grayson gives me one of those smiles that doesn't reach the eyes, the kind where the corner of the lips twitch upward in false sympathy. I give him one back, and finally relax against the door, dropping my hand from being on the verge of closing it. Naturally, the second I let my guard down a little, my phone rings at top volume in the background.

I know it's Caitlyn because she's the only one who would call this early and on this day.

"I'll let you answer that. It was nice meeting you, Maggie." The way Grayson says my name, his voice is filled with compassion, and it ever so slightly undoes the knot in my throat.

"You as well."

Grayson and his dog step off the porch and out into the sunlight as my phone's jovial jingle plays in the background. I quickly shut the door and rush through the house to my phone where Caitlyn's name is flashing on the screen. Jovi follows behind me, seemingly relieved he doesn't have to focus on the front door any longer, and I set the envelope down on the bedside table and poke the "call answer" button. "Hello, Caitlyn."

"Maggie, what took you so long?"

A typical question, as if Caitlyn imagines me doing nothing but painting and going to the beach with Jovi.

"There was someone at the door."

Caitlyn waits for me to expand on my statement, but when I don't, she fills in the silence. "That's early. Anyway, I just thought I'd call to see how you're doing and what your plans are for the day."

I flick my gaze over to the envelope, a somewhat crinkled alabaster, wondering if I should tell her about Grayson's visit this morning. Rolling the thought over and over in my head, I consider the pros and the cons, both of which happen to be the same: pro, she might want to know about the contents and not leave me alone to open it and see what's inside; con, she might want to know what's inside.

I opt not to tell her.

"Probably the same as any other day. I'll take Jovi out, work on some commissions. I have to run to House 'N Home for a few things. I don't think Taylor would want me to sit around and be sad."

What I don't say, on top of receiving the letter, is that I spend many days being sad anyway. The feelings aren't of the same deep sadness anymore, and they aren't every day, which the resource lady at the department would say constitutes "moving on." But I don't think there's much moving on I can do today, of all days.

"You're probably right. I'm going to breakfast. Taylor's favorite meal, you know. I thought I'd honor him that way, but your way works too."

As if I don't know that breakfast was his favorite. As if we hadn't been together for years before the shipwreck. As if...

I sigh, but not loud enough for Caitlyn to hear. "That's a great idea."

"Anyway, you seem distracted so I'll let you go. Try and have a good day, alright? Thinking of you."

"Thinking of you too, Caitlyn."

She hangs up without saying anything more, and I have to look down at my phone to make sure that the call has disconnected. A million thoughts cascade through my mind. Can I open this? Will I be able to survive what's inside? What if it's empty? What if the whole thing really was a joke, even though Grayson seemed so sincere?

Jovi nuzzles my other hand and I plop down on the unmade bed amid the morning glow, a combination of egg yolk yellow and dust particles and tufts of dog hair. Slipping my finger underneath the envelope's glued edge, I tear it open carefully to reveal a crinkled piece of paper. My fingers shake as I pull out the letter—or what I assume is a letter. But I don't unfold it.

I can't unfold it.

There are words in there I'm not ready to read. There are words in there that will capsize my sinking ship on a day like today. Instead, I pick up the sheets of paper and put them back on the bedside table next to the phone. Absently, I find myself looking out the window toward the dunes and the ocean and the rocks, feeling the need to be near the water on a day like this. A day to remember, but also a day with so many things I wish I could forget.

"Hey Jovi, want to go to the beach?"

I barely get the sentence out before Jovi barks once, rushing from the bedroom toward the front door with the excited *click-click-click* of his nails.

Chapter Four

It's later than usual when Jovi and I finally get to the beachfront, partially because of Grayson's visit and Caitlyn's phone call, and partially because I'm moving slow. I check the tracking on Cordelia Martin's package, see what else needs to be done on Wilhelmina Dare's small canvas, and finally get ready to head out into public. Jovi waits, a combination of patience and impatience at my delay, and when we get down over the dunes and rocks to the sand, I let him off leash and he runs to the water's edge. There's barely a pause before he throws himself into the ocean, splashing up a storm, and I can't help but smile at his excitement.

A year ago, I wasn't sure I'd ever smile again. Especially not on a day like this one, but slowly and surely, certain things are making me happy again.

I find a stick for Jovi to play with and toss it toward the water where he's hunting little crabs and diving underneath the surface. As I walk along the shore, looking out at the empty, post-sunrise horizon that's devoid of ships, Jovi slowly follows along, stepping in and out of the ocean. The sky's a pretty blue, a lighter color than the water and Grayson's eyes. For a second, I wonder why I can't stop thinking about their specific shade, but I don't get much time to consider it—or the feeling that was in my stomach when I saw them again this morning—before I spot Jovi rushing down the beach with a stick toward a vaguely familiar woman.

"Jovi! Jovi, come!" I jog toward the two figures in the distance, wondering what's gotten into him today, when I realize the woman he's galloping toward is the one from House 'N Home's paint department. "Jovi! Here!" I speed up, rushing as fast as I can across the sand that sinks underneath my sneakers.

Thankfully, the lady kneels down in the sand, picking up the stick as Jovi drops it. He sits his bum right down like he knows he's supposed to, looking back at me like he's proud of having made a new friend. Of course, he must recognize her as dogs are allowed in House 'N Home, but still. He should know better than to run off across the beach toward people at random.

"I'm so sorry!" I say as I approach the woman, trying to catch my breath and clip the lead on Jovi at the same time. "He's full of beans today. Usually, there's nobody out here when we come, but it's a little later than usual for us."

She stands from her crouched position and offers Jovi his stick, which he happily takes. "No problem, I'm a dog fan. You're Maggie, right? You were in House 'N Home the other day, talking about painting your living room wall."

"I was. You must have a good memory."

"Eastern Port's a pretty small town. It's not hard to remember everyone when you've been here a while. Especially when new folks come around. I only have to remember a couple of new names every so often, new babies and the like."

I brush a stray hair off my damp face, the heat of the day already causing me to sweat, and having to chase Jovi didn't help. I think the woman's name is Josie, but without her name tag, I can't be sure. Plus, after her innocent comment, I feel awkward bringing it up. "A little bit."

"I'm Josie, by the way. I live over on Cherry Street in the little blue house with the gate."

Oh, thank God. I don't have to ask.

Jovi cracks his stick with his teeth, interrupting the conversation to remind us that he's still being a good boy and waiting patiently for acknowledgment. I gulp down some more air and give him a pat on the head. "This is Jovi, who probably should apologize for so rudely introducing himself. I promise he's generally better behaved than this. Today's already been a bit exciting for him."

Josie smiles, pushing her dark ponytail over one shoulder. "Having a good day so far?"

I know the question can't mean anything to her, that it's honest and harmless. But I don't know how to answer because the question is threatening to make me fall apart, reminding me of Grayson and the letter waiting at home with Taylor's words written all over the paper tucked inside. It reminds me of that yellow wall that she unknowingly helped me cover, under the guise that I just wanted to change things up. It reminds me that today is a day where I'm allowed to be sad, but I don't want to bring someone else down in the process.

"Yes, thanks." I lie because it's easier than to say that today's the anniversary of my late husband's death. "How about you?"

Josie takes a deep breath in, looking up toward the sun and closing her eyes for a second. As she does so, it's like a little lightbulb goes off above her head and she peers back down at me with her eyes wide. "Oh, Maggie. I forgot. I'm so sorry. I read the article about the anniversary in the paper this morning and it didn't even click about your... Taylor, was it?"

I nod, feeling tears at the corners of my eyes. She remembers his name. Probably from all the times he ran into House 'N Home to get things for our place, supplies for renovations when we first moved in—renovations that didn't all get finished. There was a list on the fridge next to my shipping receipts up until a few months ago, back when I gave up on prioritizing house projects over my commissions.

"Yes, his name was Taylor."

She looks like she isn't sure if she should give me a hug or keep her distance, but then Josie opts for the middle option: a polite offer. "Can I— is there anything I can do to help? Do you have family or friends visiting today?"

Shaking my head, I look back down at Jovi before I reply. "No, the only family left is Taylor's sister up in Newfoundland. She's not here today. It's just me and Jovi."

Josie hums to herself for a moment as I brush my hand across my face in a valiant attempt to clear the tears from my eyes while making it look like I'm not about to start sobbing. "Do you want to be alone? I'm sorry, I probably should have asked that first. Actually, I probably should have remembered that today was the day. I'm..." She pauses and I look up to meet her gaze, concern written all over her face. "I feel right bad about you being alone here all day. Could I maybe take you out to lunch? Might help to not be alone. If you don't have plans, that is."

Normally, an offer like this from a stranger would make me feel a bit odd, but coming from Josie in a small town like Eastern Port, it just seems... normal.

I run the thought of having lunch with her over in my head, wondering if she's asking out of pity, or maybe she doesn't want to be alone either. I don't know anything about her, and she knows more about me than I would've thought possible. Or, at least, she knows about Taylor and the accident. Either way, I do my best to think quickly about her offer.

If I go home, I'm just going to be in misery over the letter, so it's probably best for me to at least try to make a connection with another human—another human who isn't Caitlyn.

Jovi's stick cracks again, and he drops it and stands, starting to get impatient. He gives a little tug on the leash before hitting me with his wet tail, leaving a water splatter on my bare legs. "I don't have plans."

A grin crosses Josie's face. "Great! How about A Cup or Two at 11:30?"

I'm thankful that she's selected somewhere I've been before so I don't have to figure out which of Eastern Port's ten streets to drive down and park on to get there.

"That would be perfect. Are you sure you don't mind?"

"I don't mind at all. I don't have many friends in town either—not anymore since everyone moved away after university. It's nice to meet someone to connect with. Kind of funny, actually, because I don't usually walk this far down the beach. I guess I just had a feeling about it today, you know?"

I let out a puff of air, smiling a little as the tears in my eyes start to dry up. "I know what you mean. One of those 'everything happens for a reason' instances?"

"Exactly what I was thinking!" There's suddenly the soft sound of vibration, and Josie looks down at her smartwatch. "Oh! I've got a phone appointment in a half-hour, so I'd better get going to make it to the house on time. But I'll see you at lunch, okay?"

I wind Jovi's leash around my hand, feeling my spirits brighten with Josie's enthusiasm and kindness. "Sounds good to me."

Josie waves goodbye before she jogs off down the beach, her ponytail swaying behind her with every bouncing movement. The sun, meanwhile, beats down on my head, and I know I need a shower, a pace around my studio to look at Wilhelmina Dare's painting again, and to feed Jovi before heading off to meet Josie at A Cup or Two.

"Come on, Jovi. Let's go home and get some breakfast."

His tail slaps against the back of my legs as we walk side by side toward the dunes, rocks, and seagrass lining the beachfront. As we come over the top of the hill, I almost expect to see Grayson appear again with his dog, but there's only a couple of cars parked on the side of the road with people—tourists, maybe—getting their things ready for a day on the sand.

Back at the house, Jovi piles his stick on the mountain of driftwood we've collected, and I let him inside first with his sandy paws to head to the kitchen. I kick my sneakers off at the front door, socks spreading sand across the floor from my impromptu jog across the shoreline, and breathe in the faint scent of paint, along with vanilla air freshener.

After hanging up the leash in the entryway, I follow the sound of Jovi pacing on the tile where he's waiting for something to eat, and feed him before I head to the bathroom to shower and get cleaned up for lunch. I figure if I wash my hair now, the heat of the day will dry it into waves, and I'll be able to use the extra time not under a hairdryer to add details to Wilhelmina Dare's painting in the studio.

I head into the bedroom to pick out an appropriate outfit for lunch when the letter catches my eye again. It's just sitting there, next to the dirty cups of water filled with remnants of paint, folded into three sections and waiting for me to read it. I ignore it for a few minutes, pulling a T-shirt and a pair of clean shorts from my dresser drawers and laying the clothing on the bed. But it's almost as if the letter is speaking to me, reminding me of the bold MAGGIE written on the front of the envelope and asking me why I haven't read Taylor's words yet.

I can't read them now, not before lunch with Josie. I can't even read them today. My little emotional boat, my grief ship, would capsize if I looked at the pages on a day that was already threatening to capsize my grief ship.

Tearing my gaze away from the paper, I quickly head into the bathroom and turn on the shower.

Later, around twenty-five after eleven, I'm just pulling into the parking lot next to A Cup or Two. I almost feel like a regular human being, my hair done and a little bit of makeup on my face, carrying a purse, and wearing something on my feet that isn't a pair of sneakers. I honestly wasn't even sure what I did with my strappy sandals until I looked in the back of the hallway closet, but there they were. I suppose this is enough of an occasion to wear them.

Sitting outside at one of the bistro tables is Josie, and she's tapping away on her phone until she notices me. She gives a little wave, presumably to make sure that I see her, and I head over to the wooden porch area.

"Hey! You came!" She almost sounds a bit surprised, like she might have thought I'd not show up. I suppose, realistically, she doesn't know me and might have thought that I was just accepting her request to be polite but with no plans to follow through.

"Hi! I did. I thought it would be a good excuse to get out of the house, you know?"

And a good excuse to get away from that letter, tempting me with probably a whole wave of sadness.

"What did you want for lunch? My treat." Josie stands up from the metal chair, picking her wallet off the top of the table.

"Oh, you don't have to do that. I'll go in with you. I wouldn't expect you to pay for me."

She waves her hand at me, gesturing for me to stay seated. "Now, I asked you to come to lunch with me, so I'll pay, no problem. You're keeping me company and I appreciate it."

I reach for my purse. "I'll pay you back; you're keeping me company too, you know. I'll have an egg salad wrap and a vanilla iced cappuccino."

"Yummy. Okay, I'll be right back."

Josie disappears off into A Cup or Two, the glass door swinging shut behind her. For a moment, I stare at the cars driving past, then I realize that I don't know what to do while I'm sitting here alone. Josie was doing something on her phone, maybe talking to someone in her family or another friend, but I don't have anyone to talk to except for Caitlyn. Even still, I pull out my phone so the other people on the patio don't think I'm just staring into space, and I tap away on the screen, checking my recently tracked packages to see if they have been updated.

It's an empty gesture because there's not really anyone on the other end. Just people who want things from me, who don't know or care about Taylor, who complain about timelines and shipping costs or the price of a custom painting.

When Josie comes back, she's carrying the drinks and two wraps on a tray. "They're both the same. Your order sounded good so I decided to get the same thing. I've never tried a vanilla shot in my iced cappuccino before, so I figured why not today?"

She sets the tray down on the table between us, and I let her select her drink and wrap first before taking mine and unfurling the wax paper on my sandwich. We eat in silence for a few moments, the eggy goodness of the wrap settling well in my stomach in combination with the cool chill of the iced cappuccino. I was hungrier than I thought, and I'm glad for something more substantial than what I've been eating lately: cereal, cottage cheese, and ready-made meals from the grocery store.

"So," Josie finally breaks the quiet, taking a sip from her straw. "Tell me something interesting about yourself. What do you do for work?"

I swallow the bite that's in my mouth and dab at my lips with a napkin from the tray. "I'm an artist. I make commissioned and pre-made paintings and sell them online in my shop."

"Wow, that's super neat!" Josie sounds impressed, leaning forward in her chair. "What kinds of paintings? Like portraits and things?"

"Mostly landscapes. I do a lot of skylines, sunrises, sunsets, that sort of thing. The last painting I finished went off to Missouri. It was a cottage scene with this really pretty pink morning sun. I'm working on one now that's a sunrise over a beach, lots of oranges and red tones, barely bigger than my hand."

"How do you get the ideas for the paintings?"

"Oh, customers send me photographs and I work off those. But for the pre-made paintings I just paint things that inspire me, scenes that I've captured on my phone or whatnot. Honestly, I haven't done any of them recently because I'm not a very good photographer and, well, I haven't been feeling that inspired."

Josie takes another sip of her iced cappuccino, and I do the same, the coffee cool on my tongue.

"I can understand not feeling motivated after what happened last year. That must have taken a big toll on your life, especially after just moving here." Josie gives me a soft smile and I nod, swallowing a gulp of coffee, not sure what to do other than bob my head in agreement. "Sorry, Maggie, I guess I should have asked if you wanted to talk about that. I just thought... I shouldn't have assumed. Tell me about your dog?"

I set the cup back on the table, watching a droplet of condensation slide down the plastic. I really do want to tell Josie about Taylor and what's been going on in my head, but I'm not sure if I can. However, as I'm thinking about it, thinking about what to say, the words just start coming out of my mouth like a flood breaking through a dam. "It's okay. I've just, I've never really had anyone to talk about Taylor with before other than the therapist at the military resource, and my sister-in-law who I'm convinced wants to make me feel like this whole thing was my fault."

"Your fault?" Josie furrows her brow.

"I convinced Taylor to follow his dreams and come here and serve in the Navy. Caitlyn—his sister—says that he'd still be alive if I hadn't pushed him. His family wanted him to stay home and finish university, but that wasn't Taylor. He was the type to travel, to see the world, you know? Strong, manly, and blunt, but kind. Dedicated."

"Sounds like he was a great person. I mean, from the times I saw him at House 'N Home, he was always friendly. Not everyone is friendly when they come into a store, even in a small town like Eastern Port. You remember the people who are nice because they're nice people, versus those who aren't."

"Yeah." I swipe at the droplet on the side of my drink before it can hit the table. "He was special, that's for certain."

"So his sister, Caitlyn, she thinks this was all your fault but she still talks to you? You're still in touch?"

"Yeah, every once in a while, she calls to remind me that I'm the reason we don't have Taylor in our lives anymore."

Josie purses her lips. "But she didn't come down here to spend the day with you on the anniversary of his death? To come to the place where Taylor lived?"

I shake my head. "Guess she didn't think it was all that important."

"Sounds like it's important to me." Josie's comment is gentle and soft, and something about it reminds me of what it's like to have someone on your side; a friend. "But maybe she's hurting too, you know. Maybe she deals with things better when she's alone."

"Maybe."

We sit at the bistro table in the noise of the lunchtime air, the sound of cars passing by in the distance and crows cawing accenting our slurping up the bottoms of our iced drinks. The temperature is warm but there's a gentle breeze off the water, one that flutters the napkin edges, but not enough to send them tumbling to the patio floor. For some time, we get deeper into conversation about Taylor, and I recall to her the moment I found out about the accident.

"It was like my heart shattered, but almost like windshield glass," I mention, flicking the straw around in my empty cup. "Like it didn't fall apart all at once, just cracked right through but stuck together. I somehow knew I had to hold it together until the men left. Then I needed to hold it together for an hour. Then a day. Then until after the funeral. Then I kept holding on and waiting for the glass to shatter until one random day it did. And I thought, 'what am I doing here?' That's the day I went and got Jovi. The day I knew I needed something more. The day I knew I couldn't be totally alone in this world."

"Sounds like you had to process a lot." Josie blinks delicately in the noon sun, adjusting her position on her chair. "Did the resource center help?"

I tell her about the grief ship, and the waves, and how now I'm in a little boat going over ripples most days. The more I open up to Josie, the less she feels like a stranger. On top of it all, the pain that's existed in my chest for a year begins to subside.

It's an hour later when I finally realize that we've been sitting here at A Cup or Two for a good part of the early afternoon, and I'm getting sunburnt and so is Josie, whose pale skin is slowly turning a bright shade of pink. Just as I think about asking if she has anywhere else she needs to be today, her smartwatch vibrates. She pokes at the screen and then looks up at me with a small frown.

"Sorry, I'm getting called into work for this evening and you're looking awfully red. Did you maybe want to pick this up another time?"

My cheeks burn hot at the sudden realization that I've just dropped a load of my life on Josie, and yet she still wants to hang out again. "Are you sure? I didn't mean to bombard you with everything that's happened to me in the last year. I just— it was nice having someone non-judgmental to get my thoughts out to."

She gathers up our trash from the table and collects it on the tray. "It's not a problem, Maggie. That's what I'm here for. That's the nice thing about a small town, sometimes. You get to know everyone. It's like a big family, if you let it be one."

"I really appreciate it. I hope you know that."

Josie stands from the table and gives me a smile. "I know."

It seems like the perfect moment for me to turn to leave, but Josie stops me as I do. "Wait, Maggie. Want to give me your number so we can text? Maybe plan another lunch or a walk on the beach with Jovi? If you want to, that is. I know I can be kind of a lot, and I don't want you to feel pressured."

"No pressure at all," I reply, and she gleefully takes out her phone from her purse as I hoist mine over my shoulder. "I'm 555-9375."

A second passes as Josie taps the screen to enter my contact information. "Got it. I'll text you later, okay? I'm gonna grab another iced cappuccino for the road."

"Sounds good to me. Thanks for lunch, and for listening to me ramble on."

She nods. "Thanks for trusting me."

Josie walks through the threshold of A Cup or Two and I step off the patio, heading back to my car with a weight lifted off my chest. However, I know that as soon as I get back in the house, the pain of that letter sitting on my nightstand is going to come back. I could stop by House 'N Home and pick up the cushions I wanted, but I don't feel like being around other people right now. I think I just need to be alone, need to go somewhere that isn't home and need to get my thoughts out about Taylor. I pull out of the lot, and aim the car for the highway out of Eastern Port and toward… anywhere else.

Chapter Five

My gold wedding band sparkles on my finger amid the July sunlight, and I look down at it every once and a while as I drive because its presence distracts me, sitting on my hand like a boulder. Even still, there's something comforting about the weight, the reminder, the way it makes my finger feel. Like it's connected with something bigger than just me and exists to keep me from floating away entirely with my thoughts of today's anniversary.

I don't have any particular goal as I drive, but there are a hundred things on my mind I'm trying to escape from. Obvious things—the letter, the memory of the house, the closeness of the ocean, and the scent of the saltwater. There aren't many places in Nova Scotia I can visit to get away from the sea, but I head inland toward The Valley's vineyards and look-offs over plowed fields. The road noise is my symphony; radio off, foot on the gas, while my ring reflects light on top of the steering wheel.

I don't need the extra noise because my thoughts are already loud enough.

Going along the empty highway at 100 kilometers an hour, I replay some of the conversation with Josie over in my head, hoping that my verbal vomit didn't turn her off from wanting to have lunch again sometime. I push that thought out of my head to make way for the other things I can't stop thinking about.

One instance stands out: the way my stomach twinged when I saw Grayson again at my front door. It was a funny sort of thing, like my heart skipped a beat but I hiccupped at the same time. I don't know what it means because I've never had a sensation quite like that before. Part of me wishes that I'd have brought up Grayson's visit, the unusual feeling that came with it, and the letter, but I had already dumped so much information on Josie that any more would have been an overload. It's an overload for me and I'm the one living it.

Cruising past signs for gas stations and small eateries, I continue until the road becomes bumpier, bridges and lanes filled with potholes not repaired from winter starting to scatter along the drive. I opt to take a random exit and see what I can find. I need to rest my mind and try and take some inspirational photos for my paintings. The sign for exit 25 shows a pictograph for a park, and I slow down to the off-ramp and follow the placards west for Martinique.

The park is only a couple of minutes down a rural, gravel road and I crawl through the tree-lined path in my Elantra, trying desperately to not bottom out the car into the path's deep ruts. Finally, I spot a clearing and an empty parking lot. I park the car underneath a tall tree with a thick trunk that provides a little shade from the heat, and hop out of the car. It takes only a second for me to nearly sprain my ankle on the rocks, remembering too late that I'm wearing my strappy sandals instead of the sneakers I usually have on my feet. Gathering myself together, I opt to walk on the grass toward the path that leads into the woods, the sound of water running from somewhere nearby echoing in my ears.

I can never get away from the water.

Heading along next to the sound of a rushing river, I'm careful of where I step in my poor choice of footwear. It takes me about three times longer than necessary to walk the path lined with blueberry bushes and tall trees, stopping to snap photos with my phone that might make good paintings. I do my best to stay off the rocky bits and mud as much as possible, but by the time I get to the next clearing, there's a blister forming on the side of my right foot.

Thankfully, the clearing leads right up to the river's edge, and I unbuckle my sandals and leave them on the grass while I stand at the shoreline and look ahead, phone in my hand. I haven't been in the water at all since before Taylor passed. Wading and swimming remind me too much of him, too much of the ocean where he spent so much time away from the house. Walking Jovi on the beach is one thing, but actually touching the water is another thing entirely.

I look down at the ring on my left hand and sigh. It's just a ring now, not a symbol, because the thing it stands for no longer exists. It's gone. Gone into the sea with Taylor's body. Gone into the sky with his soul.

Sucking in a deep and hesitant breath, I dip my toe into the river. The water is chilled but feels nice against my warm feet and sunburnt skin, and soon I find myself tentatively wading out to the middle of the narrow brook and letting it sweep over my feet and legs. Little bubbles form around me as the water droplets tumble and fall over the rocks, swirling and curling just under my knees where I stop. The clear liquid gurgles and babbles, and I frown amid my loneliness.

No wonder Taylor loved the water so much. It's like him—it can be strong, but it can be kind. It can sink a ship, but it can show compassion in quiet ripples. It can run free, it can be untamed, and it can be contained, but only temporarily. Water dissolves, disappears, evaporates—as do we all. As did Taylor.

Standing there in the middle of the water, I punch the voicemail button on my phone, scrolling through reams of past saved calls. There are only a few messages left from Taylor, and I select one and hold the device up to my ear.

Taylor's voice crackles through.

"Hi, Mags. I'm sorry if the call drops off, the connection is fuzzy and I'm sorry I can't tell you where I am or what I'm doing. You know how it is with these missions. I just wanted to call to tell you that I miss you."

An errant tear slides down my face, and, because I'm alone, I let myself begin to cry.

"I hope you're at home painting something beautiful for one of your clients, and I hope the weather isn't too bad.

It's warm here, but that's about all I can say. I hate that. I hate that I have to keep it a secret from you." Taylor's tone begins to warble, and I know that he was feeling something that he'd probably never admit to feeling. He wasn't all that open about his emotions with his words, he was more of an *actions* type of person.

"Anyway"— he clears his throat— "I'm sorry that we couldn't talk, but I'll try calling you again soon. The plan is still to be home on Christmas Eve. I can't wait to see you. Bye."

I poke the screen to end the voicemail before there's ten seconds of scratchy background noise that follows the message, nearly dropping the phone in the water. I fumble but catch it, and stand in the narrow channel of running water and allow the tears to fall over my cheeks for a few long moments. Soon, I can't see anything beyond my waterfall of tears, and I sit down on a wet and exposed rock. My shorts get soaked but I don't care because I'm too busy sobbing quietly until my heart hurts. I miss him.

I'll always miss him.

My theoretical grief boat wobbles in the wind and the waves, but I do not let it capsize. These are mild, memory tears: ones that exist for the sake of feeling comforted in my surviving guilt. Not that I could have done anything—I don't think anyone could have.

I stay there on the rock for several minutes, waiting and crying and wishing and feeling. As my heart steadies and the tears slow to a stop, I rise from my spot in the river, put on my sandals, pick up my phone, and head to the car. As

I do, Grayson's blue eyes flash in my mind, but I shove the image away as fast as I can because it's the anniversary of Taylor's death and what kind of wife am I to be thinking about another man's eyes?

Just as I arrive at the Elantra, two cars pull into the lot, and I scramble to drive away before the occupants get a look at my soaked bottom half or my post-crying, make-up-smudged face. I head through the potholes a little too fast, scraping the bottom of the car as I make my getaway.

On the way back to Eastern Port, I listen to the oldies station on the radio. It must be Sad Song Hour because every single lyric hits me hard in the heart.

Little bird, fly away with me

Take me to the sea, over the waves

Paint a picture for me with your wings

Unbound by the sky

Unbound by the blue

Unbound by my love...

It takes a little longer to get home than it did to drive away from it.

Once I park in the driveway and shut off the car engine, I gently twirl the gold band around my finger and pick a little chip of paint from its surface. Paint's the reason I picked a ring that's simple and easy to clean. Paint's the reason for a lot of things in my life.

As I walk up the path toward the house, Jovi's bark meets my ears. He knows the sound of the car by now and gets excited to greet me at the door. Someone told me once that dogs, like babies, have no sense of time or permanence. You could leave for a minute or a day and it would still seem like forever to them. You could hide behind a doorway and you would still have disappeared. Sometimes I can't help but wonder if I'm losing my sense of time as well, between the beach walks and the paintings and the trips to Eastern Port's postal outlet.

The mountain of driftwood on the patio looks like I'm attempting to make a sculpture, but all I'm really doing is bringing the ocean home one bit at a time via Jovi.

Unlocking the door, I walk into the house, Jovi's tail waggling as I kick off my sandals. I hang my purse up on the peg by the entryway and reach down to pat his head. "Outside?"

Jovi barks once, a response to my question, and I move out of the way so he can go out to relieve himself. I leave the door open as I cross toward the kitchen to fetch a drink of cool tap water, suddenly feeling jittery from the caffeine in the iced cappuccino and sitting during the drive to Martinique and back. I'm much more careful about pulling a glass from the cupboard than I was a few days earlier, and I run the tap for a moment before I stick my cup underneath and let the water swirl inside. The clear liquid has teensy bubbles that form on the surface until I turn the tap off. It reminds me of the river.

A slurp of water cools and centers me, and I head back to the front door, walking through and plunking myself down on the front step in the partial shade. Jovi's found his ball and he's tossing it up and down in the air, playing catch with himself. I watch the young dog amuse himself in the sunlight until my cup is empty and my skin starts to prickle again with heat. I call him over and we retreat back into the house, a sea breeze beginning to blow throw the windows. It feels like it might rain later.

A respite from the heat.

That evening, I feast on crackers and peanut butter from the jar while working on the rest of Wilhelmina Dare's painting in the studio. The white details require focus and attention, especially on a canvas as small as this one. When I'm finally finished to my own satisfaction, I wipe my hands on my shorts and take a step back to admire my quick work. The colors are pretty, matching perfectly with the reference photo. Getting the right shade has always been my strength.

Jovi rests in the fluffy bed by the table, watching me with half-closed eyes. He doesn't want to miss anything, but it's obvious he's tired from all the running around and playing he's done today. He's a high-energy dog, and admittedly I'm not always a high-energy person. Today's the most I've been out roaming around in a year.

Pulling my phone from the pocket of my shorts, I check the time. It's almost sunset. Normally I'd be awake long after this, but I'm already stifling yawns while my eyes feel dry and tired.

I stare at Wilhelmina Dare's small watercolor again for a minute before I turn to Jovi. "Bedtime?"

He pricks his ears up at the word and slowly stretches, ready to return to the soft memory foam of my bed and rest on the empty side of the mattress.

"Come on, then. Let's go."

I get ready for bed between the shadows of the early evening, switching out of my top and shorts into something softer and more comfortable. The letter still sits on my bedside table but I'm so tired I'm able to ignore its calling, reaching my hand over the papers to flick on my salt rock lamp and lie down on the bed amid the dull orange glow. Jovi curls up in his usual spot, making a donut shape with his body, and I reach for my phone cord to plug it in when I spot a message I must have missed; it's from a local number I don't recognize.

Unknown: Hey! Had fun today at lunch. Thanks for meeting up with me. Hope you had an okay rest of your day. Talk soon! -Josie

It's only a quarter to nine, so I tap back a response even though I'm two hours late in replying.

Maggie: I had a

I pause because I don't know what to say. I had a good day? I had a bad day? What kind of day did I even have? I mean, I cried while standing in a river in Martinique listening to old voicemails from Taylor, so one would think that's a bad thing, but it's possible that for me it was good; healing.

Maggie: I had a

The letters stare back, waiting for me to come up with something to say to Josie. I flick out of the messages application and into my photo album, looking through the snapshots I took while at the park. Perhaps I'm hoping to find inspiration for my reply.

There are a couple of good shots of the blueberry bushes lining the path, but the rest are blurry so I delete them and turn back to Josie's message.

Maggie: I had a day.

The answer looks stupid, but I hit send because I don't know what else to say to her. She seems like the type who would understand this sort of response. She responds right away with a message that's much kinder than any I've ever received from Caitlyn.

Josie: It must have been rough, huh? Anything I can do?

Maggie: I don't think so. I'm in bed now. Just want tomorrow to come so I can be one day closer to things feeling normal.

Maggie: Sorry, that probably sounds pretty dark. I don't mean it like that, I just mean that the more time goes on, the less the loss consumes my entire life.

I look over at Jovi, whose shallow snores can hardly be heard over the sound of the overhead fan. Do dogs think about death like people do? I can't imagine it's possible, but they must experience loss, they must have the cognitive ability to comprehend when something or someone is gone forever.

My phone lights up again, interrupting my internal philosophizing.

Josie: I want to say that I understand, but I can't imagine what it feels like.

I'm past the point of believing that nobody knows how I feel or what I'm going through. I know that everyone has likely had a death in their lives by the time they get to my age. But the fact that Josie acknowledges that she might not know speaks to me about the kind of character she has, even as a semi-stranger.

My fingers hover over the screen, desperately trying to think of something to say. I almost find myself wanting to comfort her, to tell her that it's alright that she doesn't understand.

Josie: I won't keep you, especially since you're in bed. But just know that you can message or call whenever you want. We'll set something up soon to get together.

Maggie: Sounds good. Thanks for checking in, I do appreciate it.

Josie: Have a good sleep!

Josie adds a little smiling emoji at the end of her message that makes me smile a bit in return. It's so strange to have someone act considerately about Taylor's passing. Caitlyn certainly doesn't, and the lady at the resource center was paid to listen to my stories. Josie's kind heart and friendly demeanor are vastly different than either of those experiences, and I start to understand why Taylor touted Eastern Port as a friendly place to live—at least according to the travel websites he read.

I tuck myself under the sheets, trying not to disturb Jovi, leaving the salt rock lamp on for a little bit of light in case I have to get up in the middle of the night. There's something comforting about the warm glow, a glow that can still be seen through my closed eyelids as I try my hardest to fall asleep.

But I don't fall asleep. I listen. There's a general hum of the house and the noise of Jovi's breathing and the sound of the sheets rustling under my toes. The ceiling fan tick-tick-ticking. My pulse in my ears, the light wind blowing through a gap in the bedroom window. So many sounds, but none of them measure up to the ones that I want to hear. Bacon crackling as Taylor cooks breakfast. The melody of him singing in the shower. His familiar footsteps falling on the hallway floorboards.

A year has passed, but even with 365 days gone by, some days it feels like I'm still on this tiny life raft trying to make it to shore.

I thumb the spot on my finger where my wedding band sits, twisting the ring around and around until I finally fall asleep. When I dream, I'm alone on the ocean shore, looking out into the horizon and waiting for Taylor's ship to come in. It feels like I'm waiting forever, cardigan pulled around my shoulders and bare feet in the sand. But soon, the sound of light rain pattering against the bedroom window wakes me and I know I've made it to another day.

Chapter Six

The gentleness of the rain comforts me. I don't know if it's from the delicate sound of the water on the windowpanes or the idea that the desperate grass is going to have some respite from the summer sun. What I do know is that Jovi wants to go to the beach despite the damp weather, and I'm more than okay with taking a walk along the shoreline because that's what we do most days of the week anyway.

I slurp down the rest of my tepid tea as Jovi munches away on his breakfast, and look over at the "sea breeze" wall as the noise of the weather and the atmosphere of the house sinks into my bones. The kitchen window is open just a bit, blowing the scent of ocean salt in through the gap and rustling the baby hairs on the back of my neck that have fallen free from my haphazard ponytail. The receipt on the fridge for the postal outlet wiggles back and forth in the breeze, reminding me that I should check the tracking at some point today and see if Cordelia Martin's painting was delivered.

Jovi gives the bottom of his empty bowl a lick before looking up at me.

"You want to go to the beach now?" The word "beach" is the key one in the sentence. I'm sure he doesn't understand the remainder of the question, but he waits until I finish speaking to bark and trot off toward the door.

Setting my mug down in the sink, I breathe in a deep sigh of ocean air before following Jovi. My black and pink sneakers slip easily onto my feet, well worn and filled with little grains of sand from all our adventures on the shore, and I grab a hoodie from the peg behind the door to hide my terrible morning hair that's only going to get worse with the humidity and the rain. After slipping my arms through the sleeves, I fetch Jovi's leash and clip it to his collar—hiding under his fluff, as usual—and open the front door to a rush of summer drizzle.

We head down the hill and across the empty street, no cars to be seen except for a black hatchback. Meanwhile, the sky is a combination of seagull gray and soggy paper white as Jovi and I cross the dunes and walk over the rocks to the oceanside. Once our feet hit the sand, he begins to wag his tail, knowing that this is the time for him to jump in the water and be free of the lead. I unclip him as quickly as possible and he takes off, happy and wiggling, across the beach toward the water, where he launches in after some birds. Watching him makes me grin, mainly because of his carefree nature. He doesn't know anything bad about the world, unlike I do. Unlike most people, I suppose.

Normally I'd take a seat on the sand after walking around, but today I sit down on the rocks at the edge of the breakwater and study the colors of the landscape. Everything is covered in a haze of rain to the point where the horizon and the ocean seem to blend together, except for where the water is lapping against the beige sand in small waves. Some of the ripples are courtesy of Jovi's furry, wet body hopping in and out and cracking across the surface, while others are the natural movements of the tide.

I don't know how long I sit there on the rocks, staring out into the grand expanse of the sky and imagining painting a gloomy portrait of the beach. But when footsteps sound from behind me, I barely have time to process what I'm hearing before a thundering German shepherd bolts past where I'm sitting and out toward Jovi, who is wading around looking for more floating sticks. I hurriedly stand up and go to call for Jovi, but before I have the chance, a man's voice calls for the shepherd.

"Perdi, come!" Someone runs along the pathway with quick but muffled footsteps. "Perdita!"

The dog stops in her tracks—more obedient than Jovi when he sees another dog—and turns back toward the man, whose frame appears from up and over the top of the dune. Jovi chooses this moment to run out of the ocean, mouth open and dribbling water from trying to catch rocks and sticks and seagulls, careening right for the shepherd as he barks up a storm.

"Jovi! Get over here!" Jovi hesitates for a moment, seemingly processing my demand, and chooses to ignore it as he picks up the pace toward the shepherd, kicking sand from underneath his paws. I trot out toward him, knowing if I run too fast he'll think this is a game and take off down the beach and it'll take me an hour to catch him.

The man runs over the rocks and jumps onto the sand, calling ahead. "I'm sorry, she doesn't usually misbehave like this!"

I know the feeling. But I also know the voice. It causes a little rumble in my stomach, like my heart is skipping a beat or I've swallowed soda too fast.

Cornering Jovi, I reach for his collar and snap on his leash as the German shepherd looks on with what I could only call amusement. I reach underneath her fur and hold on to her collar so she can't take off like Jovi would. Thankfully, she patiently waits for the man to run out and fetch her, sitting nose to nose with Jovi.

The man jogs up, taking the dog's collar, and my heart legitimately skips a beat as our hands brush. That voice was recognizable, yes, but it's his blue eyes that cause my insides to coil themselves around one another in the best way possible.

Grayson Smith.

He's standing there in front of me in a pair of khaki shorts and a tight black tee, his shoulders straining against the seams of the sleeves as he moves to take his dog from my hold. His beard and hair are closely cropped and everything about him screams that he's in the military except for the camera case he's shouldering.

"Thanks for hanging on to..." For a moment I don't seem to register to him, probably because I'm all tucked into my hoodie, the hood part scrunched up around my face. "Maggie?"

I let go of Perdita's collar and stand up, clearing my throat in an attempt to dissolve the awkwardness that's settled there. "H-hi."

"Hi." There's a pause as Grayson clips on Perdita's leash, and then he straightens as well. "Good morning. I didn't expect to see anyone else out here in the rain."

"Neither did I. Usually Jovi and I are here alone."

Grayson nods, looking down at Perdita, who has risen from sitting on the sand and is carefully sniffing at Jovi's face. I peer down at Jovi to avoid staring at Grayson, Jovi straining at his leash to get to Perdita.

"I just came out to get a few photos." Grayson lets out a muffled cough like he's trying to dispel the weirdness between us, two strangers who only met one day earlier but maybe—possibly?—have more to say than what was said before.

"Not much to take pictures of today," I note, looking up to meet those blue eyes again. They appear bright amid the morning's dismal gray. "Pretty hazy out here."

He shrugs and then offers a gentle but somewhat playful smile. "I always find something. Well, when I'm not chasing dogs or delivering letters. Speaking of letters, I didn't mean to upset you yesterday. I hope that whatever was in that envelope helped bring closure."

I loop Jovi's leash around my wrist as he and Perdita continue to sniff around. Do I tell Grayson that I didn't even bother reading it after he took time out of his day to come and bring it to me? Do I tell him that I can't bring myself to learn what it was that Taylor wanted to say to me?

"You don't have to say anything if you don't want to, Maggie. I'm sorry I brought it up."

Furrowing my brow a little, I shake my head. My heart is beating a weird rhythm in my chest and I don't know how to make it stop, but I'm also not sure I want it to stop. It's strange because I remember having a similar sensation when I met Taylor, but now? Now isn't the right time. I'm not attracted to a stranger, that would be too odd and it's too soon and it would be a betrayal of Taylor's memory... wouldn't it?

"No, it's okay. I just— I opened it but I couldn't bring myself to read it. Not yet. Maybe later."

Grayson nods a second time. "Understood. I guess it's one of those things that you don't know what's in there until you get a look at it, and you don't know if it's a good time until it's too late."

He could very well be talking about the way my insides feel, but I know he means the letter, so I bob my head. Just as I do, Jovi tugs hard on the leash to sniff at Perdita, and Perdita pulls Grayson off-balance so she can meet Jovi's nose. I nearly trip over both of the dogs, automatically putting my hands up to avoid a fall, just as Jovi jumps sideways and wraps his lead around Grayson's legs. Perdita runs forward in between the two of us and wraps her leash around me, crashing Grayson and me together. Our chests meet and my hands find a space on his arms, while his fingers locate my sides to hold me up so the two of us don't topple over in the sand or fall on top of the dogs.

For a moment, the world stops moving, and it's like Grayson and I have been careened into a careful dance with one another, two strangers stuffed in an intimate moment that neither of us is ready for. Admittedly, though I feel awkward for having been pushed into his arms, there's something safe about their broadness and warmth here in the rain. Plus, I can't untangle myself from him thanks to the leashes. I'm stuck looking up at him from under my hoodie, immediately easing my grip on his arms, melting into the blue eyes that would match the ocean on any day other than today.

"Um..." I choke out, averting my gaze that was originally locked on his eyes. When I peer down at the dogs, they're sitting on one side of Grayson and me, looking rather pleased with themselves.

"Uh, here, I'll untangle us. You stay where you are." Grayson drops his hands from my waist and, after doing a little bit of fancy footwork, steps over the curled-around leashes and frees himself. "Don't move, I'll get you out."

He unravels me from the two leads, the scent of woods and ocean surrounding me. Only one of the aromas is native to the area we're standing in now, so the woodsy smell is definitely coming from Grayson—a combination of trees and musk and vanilla. I try to suck it in without making it obvious I'm doing my best to remember it. But I swear, and I might even put money on it, that as Grayson untangles me from the final wrap of the leash, he pauses with his hand on my waist before turning me around to face him. The movement frees me, and the two of us stand there with our dogs who are more than happy to be together.

Grayson is still close, closer than a stranger would typically be, that sweet vanilla scent mixing with sea salt. It muddles into my mind like different tubes of acrylic paints, the deep chocolate brown of the vanilla and the white and blue aesthetic of the sea salt making a shimmering shade of blue-y beige. It's like the sand on a summer day, any summer day but this rainy one where the shoreline disappears into the hazy horizon.

He clears his throat, as if realizing we're in each other's personal bubbles, and takes a step back, putting a gap between us. I don't know why I don't think of moving first, but I'm frozen there with the memory of his touch seared into my skin. This also means that I have no idea what to say to break through the awkwardness, focusing more on the little sparks coursing through my veins than putting words together.

"Maggie?" Grayson says, and the deep tone of his voice gives me goosebumps along my arms and up the back of my neck. "Would you, I mean... could I trouble you to have dinner with me tonight? I want to make up for bombarding you with the letter and Perdi's bad manners today."

"Oh, it's okay. You don't owe me anything." The words come out all rushed, and suddenly the idea of standing here on the beach alone with Grayson makes me feel very exposed. I adjust Jovi's leash in my hand and try to collect myself. "We'll just go. I mean, we should go. Jovi and I, that is."

Come on, Maggie. You're better than this.

Grayson's expression dissolves into what I'd describe as a slightly disappointed frown, wrinkles showing on his forehead. "Okay, that's fine. Sorry for being presumptuous. I didn't mean anything by it."

"Don't be sorry. It's just…"

It's just what, Maggie? It's just that you're preoccupied and sinking in the blue of this man's eyes every time you see him? What's the harm in dinner? When's the last time I had a proper evening meal that didn't involve eating over the kitchen sink so I don't dirty any dishes?

Caitlyn did tell me that I should be out meeting people in Eastern Port, trying to make friends. I'm not sure this is what she meant, being tangled in leashes with an attractive—okay, I can admit that, right?—man who knew Taylor, but the advice she gave is probably sound. Plus, I has enough confidence to start talking to Josie, so what's the worst that could happen during a proper dinner with Grayson?

I realize I've trailed off and Grayson is patiently waiting for me to finish my sentence. "It's just, do you usually ask strange women from the beach on dates?"

Grayson laughs, the sound coming from deep in his throat, and I can't help but smile even though I'm truly curious about the answer.

"I didn't say anything about this being a date. Just an invitation for an apology dinner."

I smirk, then quickly wipe the expression from my face because I don't want Grayson to think I'm flirting with him. Smirking equals flirting, doesn't it? "An apology dinner sounds an awful lot like a date."

"You sound a little like you want it to be a date."

Balking, I take a half a step backward away from Grayson, beginning to toy with the wedding band on my finger. "No, no, that's not it at all, I just— I don't know. I'm used to being alone and not talking to anyone except Jovi. The dog. *My* dog. It feels strange holding a conversation where the other participant talks back."

"It's okay, Maggie. Really. I shouldn't have said anything. I don't know what I was thinking."

Grayson and I stand there on the sand, avoiding one another's gaze for a few seconds. We stare out at the horizon and then down at our dogs, who have since taken to waiting patiently and are no longer attempting to tie us together, before our glances meet and we share a small smile. At this moment, the rain picks up, the drizzle turning to a full-on rainstorm. My hoodie is soaked through before I can even open my mouth to speak, the skies opening in sheets of water that cascade over us like large waterfalls.

"I should go," I practically shout, the sounds from the storm breaking up my words like radio static.

Grayson nods roughly as rain crashes into the ocean next to us, making hard ripples. "Me too. Maybe I'll see you here again."

"Let's hope for better weather next time."

I tear myself from the conversation, looking down at Jovi and nodding back up toward the dunes. I don't have to say anything to him because he practically drags me up over the rocks and seagrass toward home. We run across the empty roadway, crossing the faded double yellow line, Jovi straining at his leash and forcing me to run faster. The knoll to the house is slick with rainwater, and my shoes squelch as I try my hardest not to slip. We make it to the driveway as thunder starts to roll and enter the house with the first flash of lightning that lights up the darkening sky. It doesn't matter though, because my clothes are drenched through and Jovi smells like wet dog because, well, that's what he is.

I tell Jovi to stay on the front doormat as I grab a towel from the bathroom to dry him off, and as I'm about to let him go and probably dampen some piece of furniture, Grayson's request for dinner replays in my mind. *Should I have accepted? I couldn't possibly. It's too soon. It would be too strange.* Excuse upon excuse floats through my mind, and finally Jovi sneaks away from the towel, leaving me by the front door amid the crackle of lightning and with dripping clothes.

Why would Grayson want to apologize for the letter, anyway? It's not like he could possibly know what's inside, and it's not like I even know what's written on the pages since I haven't read them yet. Maybe I should, though. Maybe now is the time.

I pad my way down the hall to the bedroom, my wet sock feet leaving footprints on the hardwood floor. Quickly undressing, I change into something dry—leggings and a tunic-length tank top—before re-tying my hair in a bun on top of my head. Then I sink into the covers, ignoring the permanent paint splatters on the sheets and the cups of murky paint water on the night table. Reaching over, I pick up the pieces of paper, folded over so I can't read what's written on the other side. A deep breath gets caught in my throat, like I was going to inhale and sigh at the same time.

Staring down at the pages, I toy with the corners, careful not to fold or crinkle them. A minute must go by, then two, and I still haven't opened the papers to see what is in Taylor's note. I can feel more than one page, maybe three in total, but they're small, like a thank you note from a wedding or anniversary party. I swish them under my fingers. Yes, three pages. Three separate sheets of words from Taylor that I didn't even know existed.

Maybe I'll just try reading the first page. That's what I'll do. One page today. I'll read the other pages later. Some other time. To fully absorb the feeling of Taylor being gone, but also allow myself to be present with these pieces of paper, the oil of his skin still there somewhere and mixed with mine, and maybe Grayson's too.

I unfold the sheets slowly, savoring the anticipation. As the words become clear, in front of me is Taylor's blockish handwriting, smaller than usual, probably in an attempt to squeeze as much as possible onto the small, ivory pages.

Dear Maggie —

The familiar angle of his writing sends tears to my eyes almost immediately. I choke back a sob as I examine the penmanship for a piece of him, settling with the way the words sit directly on the ruled lines, organized and proper, just like Taylor.

I hold my breath as I read.

If you're reading this, I'm gone.

I don't mean gone in the way that I'm gone to sea, or gone in the way that someone goes to the store to pick up eggs and bread. I'm gone. Really gone. And I hate it, because it likely means that I'm somewhere without you. Which is both good and bad—good because you're not gone, but bad because I'm alone and maybe so are you.

His voice resonates through my head as I read in silence, my fingertip following along the lines.

I remember being alone before I met you. Even though it was many, many years ago, those times didn't seem as bright as the times after we got to know one another. You standing there in my doorway in my leather jacket after I picked you up from a party you weren't supposed to be at, the night when everything fell into place. Things got brighter. The world had more colors. You gave me a reason to follow my dreams, even though sometimes those dreams interfered with what other people wanted from me. I'll never forget the support you gave me, a hundred percent beside me at all times.

But I don't want to focus on the alone, the gone, or the left-behind. And I don't want you to do that either. Please don't think that means you're not allowed to be sad; miss me—then let me go.

The end of the first page hits me like I've just crashed the car into a brick wall. *How am I supposed to let him go? What does he even mean by that?* I begin to feel overwhelmed with questions, ones that I know the answer to already and others that I don't, ones that hurt and others that make me curious. My heart hurts, my head hurts, my whole body begins to ache with the effort of holding in my sobs.

How long?

How long until I'm not allowed to miss him anymore?

How long until I have to let him go?

I fold the paper over into threes again, forcing myself not to read the other pages because just this one has given me enough heartbreak for a day. For a week. For long enough that I'll need to figure out the math and hope for a statistical response to the time it takes to get over someone's sudden death. And then, once I get some vague number, I'll have to tack on months and years because that person who died was my soul mate and I'll never find a love like that again. There must be some kind of equation for this. Some formula to getting over loss. Maybe I could call the resource therapist and ask. Maybe I could Google it. Someone must know. There has to be an answer.

A tear drops onto the back page of the note and I swipe it away so it can't soak through and smudge the black ink. Rain falls outside, like the sky itself is crying. And as I set the letter from Taylor back down next to the cups of paint water and then lie back on the bed, I let myself curl into Taylor's permanently empty spot on the mattress and breathe in the scent of laundry, emptiness, and feather pillows.

Chapter Seven

I don't make it to the postal outlet to mail Wilhelmina Dare's painting until the next day, because I've holed myself up in the bedroom with Jovi, the sound of the rain, and thoughts of the first page of Taylor's letter. It thunders off and on throughout the afternoon and evening, just enough time in between rumbles that I'm able to wonder if the storm is over—and then a distant echo sounds to remind me that the bad weather persists.

Josie texts me, but I don't feel like talking, so I don't bother opening the message to see what it says.

I do manage to get up to eat something around seven at night; a spoonful of peanut butter over the sink as the wind blows the scent of salt through the kitchen. The taste of the ocean nearly catches on the pasty brown glob, and I lick absently at it until the dollop disappears. Setting the spoon down in the empty sink, I retreat back to the bedroom, falling asleep to the rain and the wish for Taylor yellow skies.

When I wake, the weather is bright and dewy, and I find myself in a better mood than I was after reading the note's first page. It makes me wonder if I really should be exposing myself to the heartbreak that I was just starting to wean myself off from, but then I feel bad about the thought of not finishing what Taylor took the time to say. Maybe with the next page, I'll be more prepared.

Jovi's still lounging around and dozing, so instead of taking him for his morning walk right away, I head down to my studio. Bundling up Wilhelmina Dare's small painting and completing the customs forms online, I sign the bottom and the back of the canvas before heading into the main living space and kitchen.

Josie's message is still showing as unread, so I pop it open and read her text.

Josie: How are you doing? Thought I'd check in real quick. Let me know if there's anything I can do to help.

Maggie: Hey! All good here. Thanks for the note. Just heading to the postal outlet. Might pop by House 'N Home later to pick up some cushions for the studio if you're working?

Josie: I'll be there after eleven. See you then!

I slip on my sandy sneakers and, after saying goodbye to Jovi, who is still in the bedroom, I head out into the glistening morning. The car is covered in droplets from the day before, the sun not yet having had the chance to burn off all the moisture in the air. I unlock the doors and take a seat, placing the package on the passenger's side, before backing out of the driveway and onto the main road.

The drive to the postal outlet only takes a couple of minutes, and when I get there, only one car is in the lot: a black hatchback. At least there won't be a long wait or a line, and I make a mental note to check on Cordelia Martin's tracking when I get home. Lifting the package from the seat, I open the car door without looking. Much to my terrible luck, I nearly hit a man walking past me toward the other vehicle.

"Oh! I'm sorry! I wasn't looking..." I immediately fall into a cycle of apologies, feeling awful for not paying attention to what I'm doing or where I'm going.

The man leans down and his blue eyes catch me almost off guard but not off guard enough. It's like I subconsciously expected to run into Grayson Smith again at some point—it was just a matter of when.

"Hi, Maggie." His fingers wrap around the top of the car door, and he holds it open for me to step out into the sun that's suddenly gotten way too hot. I'm glad that at least this time I've managed to do something with my hair and I'm kind of properly dressed—unlike yesterday at the shore when I was a damp and unshowered mess.

"Hi." I don't know what to say, so that seems like a good start. *What is it about his eyes that always captivates me?* "What are you doing here?"

Grayson's lips twitch, like he wants to laugh but is trying to hold it in. "I had a package to mail. That's what people often come here for."

"Right. Um—yeah." I mentally facepalm myself for asking such a stupid question. Why else would he be here?

"I take it you're mailing something too then?" The question is gentle, attempting to guide me into some semblance of a conversation that doesn't revolve around inquiries that are much too obvious.

"Yeah." I hold up the unsealed envelope with the painting tucked inside. "Business package."

"You have a business? What do you do?"

Grayson genuinely sounds interested, which is sweet but also makes my heart beat faster for some strange reason. However, work is something that's easy for me to talk about, so I quickly fall into my regular pitch for my business. Of course, I couldn't possibly get the words out properly and sound like I know what I'm talking about because that would be too easy. Instead, I stumble over explaining, going into a bit of a ramble to get all the details in.

"I'm an artist. I make commissioned paintings for people from all across the world. Lots of landscapes. Different sizes. Mostly watercolors. It's fun, at least the majority of the time. I also try to find time to paint the things that I want to paint and pop those up on my shop site, but, uh, it's been a little difficult for the last going off to feel inspired outside of other people's photographs."

He flicks his gaze down to the envelope I'm holding, then back up at me. "I'd love to see that. I do photography in my spare time, so I'm always interested in creative interpretation of different artistic mediums."

"It's not sealed yet. I can show you, if you want?" I don't know why I offer because I'm nervous as anything to show Grayson my work. What if he's a really good photographer and thinks that my watercolor canvases are amateur garbage? I know it's imposter syndrome speaking, but as hard as I try to suck the words back into my mouth, they're already out in the world.

Grayson folds his arms atop the car door between us. "That would be amazing."

I reach my hand into the envelope and carefully draw out the small canvas. The painting practically sparkles in the sun, the colors bright, and a smile breaks over Grayson's face as he examines my work.

"Wow… Maggie, that's beautiful. I definitely understand why people order custom work from you."

My face prickles with heat, not from the sun but from the compliment, and I tuck the painting back in the envelope with the reference photograph. "Oh, this one isn't much. I did one earlier in the week that was larger and had this beautiful pink sun. It went to Missouri and almost didn't need a painting, you know? The picture was just about perfect."

"What did they think? The person you painted it for, I mean?"

"Still waiting on delivery. I'm hoping they leave a good review when it arrives though."

For a moment, Grayson and I don't say anything, our gazes averted even though they meet for a second or two and then flit away. His fingers drum on the edge of the car door where he's leaning, and I shift my weight so I'm pressed up against the back passenger door. Even with my distance from him, that musky vanilla scent still permeates the air around us. Someone once told me that smell is one of the strongest senses for nostalgia—and I'd have to believe them. Every scent of breakfast reminds me of Taylor, pancakes mainly, but this vanilla warmth mixed with the ocean is distinctly Grayson.

"Listen, Maggie—I'm sorry about yesterday. I feel like I'm saying I'm sorry a lot, but I wasn't thinking when I asked you to dinner. That wasn't very considerate of me."

I shrug a little, offering a smile. Part of me wishes I would have taken him up on it because my spoonful of peanut butter from last night is long gone. "That's fine. I guess it just took me by surprise. I've never, Taylor... life kind of revolved around him, you know? I mean that in the nicest way. It's still strange to think about not having him around."

"I get that. I'm..."

"You don't have to keep saying that you're sorry, Grayson. Everyone is always sorry. And honestly, I kind of liked that you asked about dinner. Because my sister-in-law has been bothering me to get out of my house for some time now.

I don't know if she's serious or not but the offer was kind, even if it felt a little weird to consider it."

"But you did consider it?"

I nod, running my free hand through my hair and shielding my face from the sun. "In an awkward way, I suppose that I did. It just... it feels like betrayal. It feels like I'm not supposed to."

Grayson's lips twitch in a little, sympathetic smile. "Some day you might change your mind. And that's not meant to try and pressure you—it's meant more as comforting words. Though I can see how it would be taken the wrong way. And... maybe I should just stop talking. I'm probably digging myself into a hole."

"That's what the resource therapist told me. That the grief will dissolve little by little. And it has. It's just when things happen, like the letter... Those things wash waves of sadness all over me again."

"That sounds like you read it." He gives me a look to imply it's a question.

I blink into the sunshine, looking at the cars driving along the highway in the horizon. The sky is a perfect blue with puffy white clouds, one that I might be able to paint if I used just the right brushes. I could snap a photo with my phone but it wouldn't do the clarity justice.

"I read the first page," I reply, reaching forward for the car door to shut it. Suddenly there's nothing between Grayson and me, no physical barrier, and I'm able to get a better look at his tall stature, thick thighs, and broad chest. "I... I have feelings about it."

"Maybe it will get easier?" Grayson bites at his lip for a second as I toy with the edge of the envelope.

"Maybe. I hope so."

"When are you going to read the rest of it?"

"I don't know." I scuff my sneaker on the edge of a pothole in the driveway. " Once I've processed the first page, I guess. There are two more pages I can't imagine what Taylor would have written on them."

"It's kind of sad and beautiful. The thought of a letter a year later. Like he means to keep thinking of you even though you're here and he's... not."

"Yeah. I suppose. Right now, it's mostly just heartbreaking, but maybe later it'll be less of a shock." *Maybe I'll get numb to it, like freezing cold ocean water.*

Grayson chuckles softly. "I don't think you get over it—I think it just becomes part of you."

He pulls his car keys from his pocket, pressing the key fob to unlock the hatchback's doors with a beep. So, it's his car. The sound brings me back to our surroundings: the postal outlet, the sky, standing together in this parking lot like kind of infinite dance of serendipitous meetings. I wonder why fate has us continuing to run in to one another. There must be some reason, a reason that spans more than both of us living in the same tiny town. I don't know why I believe this, but a wiggling feeling in my stomach tells me that Taylor has a plan for us.

"Grayson?"

He hums a response, looking down at me while bathed in sunlight and shadow.

"I was thinking of cooking chicken parmigiana for supper if you'd be interested." I haven't made chicken parmigiana in a year, but there's no reason he has to know that. I also haven't had anyone over to the house in a year, but he doesn't have to know that either.

"I thought that..."

I hold up my hand that's not clutching Wilhelmina Dare's package, and Grayson pauses. I already know what he's going to say, something about my earlier comment of betrayal or pain or loss or whatever else I've told him. However, my gesture stops him, and I'm glad because I honestly don't know how to answer the question of what changed my mind. Maybe I'm just tired of being alone every night, and maybe I'm trying to live by Taylor's words—miss him, but let him go.

"You don't have to decide now, just... if you want to come, I'm at 11 Marigold. Maybe around seven?" *What time do people do these kinds of things at, anyway?* I have absolutely no clue what kind of hole I'm digging myself into, or if I'm even going to be able to function while having a dinner guest. Especially a man. Especially *this* man.

Grayson nods, hesitates, and then nods again. "I can do that. I'd actually really like that."

A smile creeps across my face as I tuck a strand of hair away from my cheek. "Me too."

"I'll, uh, I'll let you get your package mailed." He fiddles with his keys as if he doesn't know what else to say, as if surprised that I've actually agreed to a belated dinner with him. "But I'll see you at seven."

"Perfect."

Grayson walks past me toward his hatchback, that scent of musk and vanilla on the breeze as he goes by. I hold my fake confidence until he's in his car and I can deflate and shuffle into the postal outlet with Wilhelmina Dare's painting. My mind is reeling with thoughts and surprise errands to run—going to the market, stopping to see Josie like I said I would, cleaning the house of husky hair—and suddenly seven doesn't seem far enough away.

Plus, there are other questions on my mind. Questions about what tonight means and what Grayson expects from it. He's a military man, presumably a single one, maybe with a girl in every port, as the saying goes. *Will he expect sex? Would I give it to him if he asked?* I have needs and wants and thoughts and desires that have melted long ago into ice cream on a hot summer sidewalk; but would sex with someone new make me forget about Taylor? Would it wobble the boat in the harbor that I'm currently floating on?

I nearly trip going up the steps into the postal outlet, and before I know it, I'm back at the car and pulling out from the parking space. My whole interaction while mailing Wilhelmina Dare's package is a complete blur, and I'm in front of House 'N Home to pick up my cushions and say hello to Josie before I've totally come around and can focus on something other than, well, *that*.

Stepping into House 'N Home, I'm blasted with air conditioning, goosebumps forming on my bare arms. The housewares section is on the way to paint, and I easily find the cushions I was looking for to redecorate the studio. I tuck them under my arms and head to Josie's department. She sees me coming as she's returning paint swatches to the large wall and smiles.

"You look different." She sticks the remaining purple swatches in her apron pocket before picking off a bit of paint from her hands. How she manages to get rid of it all at the end of the day is a mystery to me, as I'm constantly covered. "And I like those cushions. The neutral color is pretty with the driftwood buttons."

"What do you mean, different?"

"I don't know." Josie shrugs. "You look happy. Not that you didn't look happy at lunch the other day but this is more like a glowy kind of happy? Your cheeks are all pink."

I bite the inside of my cheek. Should I tell her about Grayson? "I probably put on too much blush today. The light in my bathroom isn't the best."

Josie rolls her eyes. "Oh, please. What's really going on? I know we haven't known each other that long, but you're like an open book in the emotions department."

"That's just because you're easy to talk to."

"I know." She smiles at me before lowering her voice a touch so nobody can overhear. "Now tell me what's going on."

Sucking in a deep breath, I look around the paint department, checking to make sure nobody's listening. "I sort of, I don't know. There's this man. He delivered a letter a couple of days ago that Taylor wrote to me before he died. Now we keep running into one another and it's like, awkward but not awkward? I don't know what to make of the whole thing. It seems like fate, or it would if I believed in it."

"Oooh. Well, that's something. Are you going to do anything about it?"

"He asked me to dinner, but I said no."

"Maggie!"

"But then today I ran into him at the postal outlet, just before I came here. And I asked him to come over for chicken parmigiana tonight. Which wouldn't be so bad if the house were clean and I had the ingredients to make it."

Josie laughs, leaning against one of the shelf posts, her cheekbones shining with sparkly gold highlighter under the artificial light. "It's less about the meal and more about the wine. Get a couple of bottles. It might help you relax."

I hesitate, chewing on the corner of my lip, before hoisting the cushions under my arms. "Do you think that this is wrong?"

Josie reaches out and touches my arm softly. "Maggie, I don't think Taylor would expect you not to see anyone ever again."

"I'm not seeing him, it's just dinner."

She opens her mouth to say something more, but the little metal bell at the paint counter dings. "I've got to get back. But let me know how it goes, okay?"

"I will."

"And I need to know more about this letter. But not here. Text me tomorrow!"

Josie flits off toward the paint counter, and I'm left alone by the swatches with two pillows under my arms. I stand there and stare at the wall of paint for a minute, thinking about what she said regarding wine, before I shake my head, laugh to myself, and head to the checkout counter. Maybe I am too easy to read, but maybe it's because nobody's been around to read me in awhile. Caitlyn doesn't count because she couldn't possibly care any less than she already does.

Stuffing the pillows into the back seat of the car once I've checked out, I take the long way to the market, pick up some chicken, fettuccine noodles, and a frozen cheesecake for dessert, and—only with a little hesitation—pop in to the liquor store for two bottles of wine. Just in case. Not because I need it, but because Josie might have a point. I swear the lady ringing up my purchases must be judging me as my regular grocery order happens on Tuesdays and consists of things like peanut butter, cottage cheese, and dog food, but I shake it off as my imagination running wild.

I get back to the house at the exact second my phone rings, Jovi barking at my arrival, and I drop my shopping bags on the floor to finagle the device out from my tote. It's Caitlyn, because of course it's Caitlyn. She's like a mind reader of inconvenience.

"Hi, Caitlyn. How are you?" Jovi bounces in front of me, clearly ready to head to the beach to work off some of his excess energy. I almost forgot that a walk would need to fit into this afternoon, around cleaning and food preparation and possibly pouring myself some wine to calm my nerves.

"Hello, Maggie. Just checking in. You sound busy."

Jovi knocks the grocery bag over with a paw, a bottle of wine thunking against the floor but thankfully not breaking.

"Just got home with some groceries. Literally just walked in the door."

"It's not Tuesday," Caitlyn notes, her voice matter-of-fact as if she's pleased to have uncovered something about my personal life, even though I've passed on literally no information. "You having a party or something?"

Shit.

"No party. Just needed a couple of things."

Caitlyn's side of the line is quiet for a couple of seconds as I pick up the bags from the floor, trying not to trip over Jovi. I place everything on the kitchen island, trying to hold the phone with my shoulder so I can use both hands.

"I don't think I've ever heard of you running to the store because you need a couple of things. Is everything okay?"

Caitlyn doesn't really care if everything is okay. At least, I don't think she does because she never has before. She's probably trying to catch me in the middle of something else she can hate me for, which is technically exactly what she's done.

"Things are fine. Like I said, just needed a few things."

Another pause, and I lean against the counter while waiting for the conversation to continue. I can feel the time ticking away, giving me less and less of it to prepare for Grayson's arrival.

"Well, I guess it's good you're getting out of that house a little more. Even if it's just to head to the grocery store twice a week instead of once." Something on end of Caitlyn's line crinkles, like she's eating a mint or a hard candy while talking to me. It's a nervous habit of hers that she's had since we moved away, though usually I don't hear her unwrapping anything while we're in one of our conversations.

"I also went to pick up cushions, and to the postal outlet."

"Busy day." Her voice is flat and uncaring, and for a second, I debate asking her why she's bothered calling if she's not even going to try to have a real discussion. I wonder if I should tell her about the letter. It seems like the right thing to do—and may be a way to connect over something more than my sudden need for groceries.

"I got a letter. One of the guys from the dockyard dropped it off the other day. From Taylor."

"What do you mean you got a letter from Taylor?" Caitlyn's voice picks up, piquing with curiosity. She almost sounds like the old version of Caitlyn—happy, bubbly, free-spirited.

"I don't know, he must have written it in case anything ever happened to him. I thought it might have been a joke at first, but when I had a look at it, it was definitely Taylor's handwriting."

"Well, what did it say?"

"I only read the first page."

"And what did it say?" Caitlyn pushes, and suddenly I wish I hadn't told her about the letter at all. The contents feel so personal that I don't want to share them with her. They weren't meant for a sister, but I don't know how to get that message across without making her mad.

"It was... I don't know. It feels intimate. Like I'm seeing something of Taylor I thought I'd never see again."

Caitlyn barks out a laugh, just a little too loud. "Oh, don't be selfish. If he had last words for you, I'm sure the letter had last words for everyone else in his life."

By everyone else, Caitlyn clearly means her. There's nobody else besides the two of us.

"Maybe there's something on the other pages I haven't read yet." I sigh, suddenly feeling agitated. I toy with the cap of one of the bottles of wine and wonder how early I can start drinking it without becoming completely inebriated before Grayson arrives. "Listen, I've got to go. We'll talk soon, okay?"

I can almost hear the moment when Caitlyn puts the pieces together. I don't know how she does it because I don't think I've made it obvious, but the wheels turn in her head and she asks me, "Are you having dinner with someone?"

"What?"

"You heard me. Are you having dinner with someone?"

I don't have an answer prepared because I didn't think the need for one would come up. And what's it to her if I have someone over for dinner? For all she knows, it could be a friend, like Josie. Though, the issue with that is Caitlyn has no idea Josie exists, and a small idea that some letter-delivering stranger from the Navy does.

My silence goes on too long as I try to think up a response, and Caitlyn laughs that same forced laugh again. "Well, at least you're making *friends*. What's his name?"

"I'm hanging up now. I'll talk to you later."

Caitlyn, of course, gets the final word in and she chooses words that sting deep down to my bones. "You know, a year isn't very long, Maggie."

I tap the red "end call" button and set the device down on the counter before counting backward from ten to try and control my frustration. Even still, Caitlyn's words echo in my head: *a year isn't very long, a year isn't very long, a year isn't very long*. I do my best to shove them out of the way, ignoring the groceries on the counter, and look out the kitchen window at the water.

Maybe I'm making a mistake.

But then again, maybe I'm not.

Chapter Eight

Chicken parmigiana isn't exactly the hardest thing to make, but I haven't cooked an actual meal for months. My skills in the kitchen have deteriorated into practically nothing other than running around trying to make sure the noodles don't boil over and ensuring I remembered to take the cheesecake from the freezer. Every time I have a moment where I think that the dessert needs to come out to thaw on the counter, I turn and it's already there. I'm glad I didn't decide to cook a cheesecake because with the trouble I'm having, I'd have been in a real mess.

On the bright side, I managed to tidy up the house throughout the course of the afternoon, curl my hair, and put on an outfit that's a little nicer than a raggedy old tank top and jean shorts, which is success in some ways. However, once I splatter tomato sauce on my tee and have to go change, I wonder if I'm trying a bit too hard. Maybe I should just order a pizza. Or maybe, in some alternate universe, Grayson won't show up.

My heart sinks a little at that idea, and the sensation is odd because I haven't felt it in a long time. Well, at least not a year, which, as Caitlyn said, isn't all that long.

But it feels long. It feels like forever some days. Three hundred and sixty-five days. Three hundred and sixty-five years. Sometimes I think they're the same thing. But on days like today, bright days complete with sunshine and the smell of salt and seaweed in the air, I almost feel like my grief boat is floating peacefully along, and that the resource therapist would be pleased with my progress.

The two bottles of wine I bought earlier are on the island counter, one red and one white—chilled—with ancient wine glasses next to them that I had to wash the dust out of. I'm just unscrewing the top to the white, thankful that I didn't buy anything that was bottled with a cork, when I hear a car coming up the driveway. Jovi barks once to alert me, trotting over to the door as I smooth my shirt and wipe a bead of sweat from my neck, all before turning down the heat on the bubbling pot of noodles and poking the screen for the oven temperature to "off." The food ought to be done by now, and as Josie said, the wine is more important.

Footsteps come up the porch stairs, and then there's a double knock at the door. For a second, I think I might faint, a million thoughts running through my head. *What am I doing? Am I betraying Taylor? What does Grayson feel? What is it that I feel besides some kind of... attraction?* Jovi's second bark interrupts my line of questioning, his head poking through the living room curtains in an attempt to see who is waiting outside. I take a deep breath and hold it in my lungs as I cross the room, placing my hand on the knob.

You can do this, Maggie.

I release the breath and replace it with a smile as I twist the door open.

"Hey! You made it!"

Grayson's standing there in a tight blue dress shirt, unbuttoned at the neck, and a pair of jeans that are sufficiently tailored so that I can make out the curvature of his thighs. In his hand is a bottle of white wine with a beachy label on it, the outside covered in condensation droplets from the warmth. Jovi waggles his fluffy tail back and forth, excited to see Grayson again, even without Perdita. The husky barely gives Grayson a chance to walk through the threshold and onto the front mat before he dances from paw to paw for attention. Grayson hands me the bottle of cold wine before kneeling down to say hello to Jovi and dispel some of the dog's energy.

"I wouldn't have missed it. It smells nice in here." He stands after a moment and slides off his shoes by the front door, Jovi taking off down the hall, probably to find a toy to bring Grayson in an attempt to play. Not that we have visitors often, but he pulls the same stunt with repair people, who frequently oblige.

"It's nothing much but a thank you. For the letter, I mean."

Grayson nods, taking in the sights of the small, open-concept house. "Well, I'm here as a thank you as well, then. Thank you for not getting mad about Perdita's lack of manners on the beach yesterday."

Jovi suddenly appears from down the hall and careens around the couch with a stuffed pig in his mouth. He presents the disgusting toy to Grayson, who smiles and takes it from Jovi before tossing it in the air for the dog to catch.

I shift my weight. "Well, I could say the same to you about Jovi, but we're both dog people so I think we understand."

"Definitely."

Grayson tosses the pig for Jovi again, who takes the stuffed creature and runs off toward the couch with it. It's then that I realize we're still standing by the entry, awkward as anything, and I step back and wave my arm toward the kitchen. I have forgotten that the beach wine is in my hand and I nearly launch it across the room, catching myself at the last second.

"Food's ready. I just need to drain the pasta." I move out of the doorway and walk into the kitchen, Grayson following close behind as I open the fridge and place his bottle of white wine inside to stay cold. "The white is already open if you want to pour."

I'm talking so fast that I'm forgetting to breathe, my pulse pounding in my ears as I try not to show how nervous I am. I turn toward the stove to switch off the burner knob.

"How about we have a glass of wine and then dinner? I'd love to just… talk. Relax a little." He hesitates on the last part of the sentence like he doesn't quite know how to get the words across. Thankfully, when he says it, I'm facing the kitchen window, grabbing for the pasta pot to drain the noodles into my colander, so he can't see my twitchy grin.

When I turn back around, noodles drained into the pot, Grayson's poured us both wine and he slides one glass across the counter toward me. I pick it up without pause and take a sip, the taste of peaches and floral essence covering my tongue. I probably grip the stem harder than necessary, but my hands are shaking and I'm desperately trying to hide it.

"Cheers, then." Grayson tips his glass toward me with a twinkle in his blue eyes before he takes a taste of his own. I can't help but notice how his throat bobs as he swallows, but I quickly avert my gaze so he doesn't catch me staring.

"Should we go sit in the living room?" I nod toward the "sea breeze" wall where Jovi's made himself comfortable with his pig on the small couch. Admittedly, I'm not sure what to do with this man in my house other than fill the silent gaps and also feed him. "Or I can give you a tour of the place—not much to see, really. This is most of the house, plus a couple of bedrooms and my studio."

"I'd love to see your studio."

"Really?" I accidentally sound bewildered when I mean to sound thankful, because I can talk about art for hours. What I can't do is figure out how to make this whole interaction not turn awkward when we run out of small talk. I'm not good at small talk.

"Of course." Grayson smiles. "Lead the way."

I escape from behind the counter with my wine glass, heading down the narrow hallway toward the back of the house. It's shadowy along the corridor, small outlet lights guiding me, even though I could find my way around the house in pitch black if I had to. When we reach the doorway to the studio, the two of us stand there in the summer sun as I push the partially closed door open.

It's a pretty time of day in the studio, the walls awash with outdoor lighting and the windows gleaming with dog nose prints and detritus from the rain. Everything is in the place I've always left it: cups of water, paints, Jovi's extra dog bed, and the new pillows I just bought. The easel is empty of any art at the moment because I've just mailed off Wilhelmina Dare's piece, but I bet when I look in the morning on my online platform there will be something brand new to start.

I step into a patch of early evening sunlight, looking around the familiar room. "This is where the magic happens."

Grayson chuckles, walking toward the window seat where my new cushions are proudly displayed. The old pillows are hidden behind the guest room bed's headboard. I'll get rid of them eventually, but today was spent on more important things like making myself presentable and trying to avoid drinking a bottle of wine by myself before seven at night due to my nerves.

"You have a great view here, right down to the ocean. You must be able to see all the ships come in through the harbor when the sky is clear."

I nod, taking a sip of my wine, not moving from the sunny spot in the middle of the floor. "Yeah, I can. It's a pretty nice feature, most of the time."

"What do you mean, most of the time?"

Hesitating, I bite the inside of my cheek before I respond. "Well, sometimes I don't want to be reminded of ships and what can happen on them."

Grayson stares out the glass for a few moments and we are encased in the kind of silence that makes me wonder if I'm supposed to say something. Thankfully, he turns back to face me before I open my mouth and spit out something irrelevant. "What painting are you working on now?"

"Nothing in particular. I just mailed off my last commission. I'll check my inbox in the morning to see if there's something new. If not, I can always try to put together an original, though that's admittedly been pretty difficult lately. I'm not great at taking photos and you're not really supposed to copy what you find on the internet."

He hums for a moment, so low that I hardly hear the sound. "So, you need original photography?"

"That would be preferable." I shrug, another sip of wine going down my throat before I notice that my glass is already half empty.

"I, um, I have some photos from the other day I could send to you if you'd like? Maybe one of them would inspire you into putting together another original for sale?" Grayson hesitates like he's not sure if the questions are too forward or too strange. I realize that he's possibly just as nervous as I am. At least with the letter, he was able to deliver it and leave. Now, he's been invited into the house and maybe he feels trapped and like he can't go without seeming rude.

What if he wants to leave? Would he say anything?

"Maggie?"

I jolt back to the real world, nearly spilling the leftover wine in my glass as I jump. "Sorry, just thinking. I'd love to see some photos. I'm sure there's a snapshot in there that I'd want to try and paint."

"I'd show you on my phone but that probably isn't large enough. I can always email them to you? The quality will be better from the camera." He eyes the laptop and printer in the corner of the studio, the machine always on, though the display is dark.

I nearly choke on my mouthful of wine, the last of the glass. I don't know why I do because Grayson insinuating that he needs my email isn't the biggest deal in the world even though my mind and my heart are making it out to be. "Sure. Email away."

Grayson doesn't outright ask for my email address, and like the idiot I am, I don't think to offer it. Instead, I just stand there in the studio with my empty wine glass and a foggy head, wondering what in the hell I was thinking, inviting a man over for dinner.

We look around the room for a moment, taking in the sunshine and the mess of paints and supplies, before I clear my throat. "So, tell me about yourself? I mean, that's not a question, but I'd like it if you told me."

He smiles, taking a final draw from his wine glass. "How about we fill up our wine and go keep Jovi company in the living room? I'm happy to tell you anything you want to know."

Nodding once, I turn on my heel and lead Grayson back out of the studio toward the kitchen, where he fills up our glasses about an inch from the top. I eye him for a second, remembering vaguely that wine is usually served only half a glass at a time, but he smiles as if he understands my funny expression.

"Now we don't have to get up as often."

I can't help but laugh, and I follow him through the open concept dining room into the living area where Jovi's still on the loveseat with his stuffed pig. Grayson takes a seat at one end of the big couch and I find myself at the far other end facing the "sea breeze" wall, giving us a whole cushion in between to dispel some of the awkwardness.

"So, you have questions?" Grayson licks a droplet of wine from his bottom lip, which temporarily distracts me. I have to give my head a little shake in order to focus on what he means before I remember that I made a comment only minutes ago in the studio. *Shit. Now I have to think up things to ask him, things that aren't weird, things that don't sound like I'm too interested in what tonight means so I don't seem obsessed with what this all means.*

"Sure, I mean, I can think up some? I feel like it's a bit odd to have dinner with someone and not know much about them, especially when they're in your house."

"And you keep running into them randomly?" Grayson's eyes twinkle playfully in the fading sunlight as he runs a finger along the stem of his wine glass.

I allow the smirk toying at the corners of my lips to cross my face. "Well, there's always that."

"Ask away."

There's a pause then, and I wrack my brain as quickly as possible for things I want to know about him, but a million things come to mind and all of them could be misconstrued as prying into his personal life or like I'm overly interested or maybe as if I'm desperate for companionship. I settle on one of the things we have in common—the dogs. "Where did you come up with the name Perdita?"

Grayson chuckles. "That's not the kind of question I was expecting, but I suppose it's a good start."

"What were you expecting?"

"Where'd you grow up, what's your father's name and what's he do, why'd you join the Navy, that sort of thing."

I let out a little laugh. "We can get to those next if you want."

"I have a feeling I'm going to like your questions more than those standard ones. But just to get them out of the way, I grew up in Saskatchewan, my father's name was Doug and he was a carpenter, and I joined the Navy because it was about as opposite to Saskatchewan as I could get." He punctuates the answers by twirling the wine glass in between his fingers.

"And Perdita?"

"Perdita was born in Ontario, her father's name is Finnigan..." Grayson's lips quirk up in a little half-smile as he trails off. I let out a chuckle, the feeling from laughing putting me at ease as I sink farther into the couch cushions. "I'm kidding. Perdita was the name of the mother dog in that Disney movie, *101 Dalmatians*. What about Jovi? The only other Jovi I know of is Jon Bon."

"Amusingly, that's who he's named after." I slurp down more wine, trying to be careful not to spill any on the couch since the liquid is so close to the rim. "Jon Bon Jovi the dog. Taylor and I used to listen to a lot of his music."

Grayson nods. "Maybe we should keep this light—we don't have to talk about Taylor if you don't want to."

"It's okay. I don't mind. Honestly, it's kind of nice to have someone to talk to. Caitlyn—my sister-in-law—isn't the easiest person to have a conversation with."

"Why's that?" He shifts his weight on the cushion as Jovi hops off the loveseat, dropping his pig on Grayson's lap. Grayson tosses the stuffed animal for him, and Jovi trots off for a moment before returning for more.

"I..." I think about telling Grayson a lie, telling him that I don't know why she isn't easy to discuss things with, or that she's just a hard person in general. I don't know why the thought crosses my mind but I push it away and decide to be honest, like I was with Josie. "She believes that his death was my fault. That I pushed him into the Navy. That he'd still be alive if I told him to stay home and if we hadn't been posted here."

There's silence, Jovi waiting for his pig to be thrown and Grayson looking down into his wine. "I hope you don't believe that, Maggie. There's nothing you could have done."

I don't know what to say, so I just absorb what's going on around me. The pig is tossed. Jovi trots away. An awkward feeling settles in my chest. Grayson sighs.

"But how do you know?" I ask the question in a small voice, one so tiny that I'm not sure Grayson can hear me. But he leans forward on the couch, wine between his hands, fingers twitching like he wants to reach out and touch me but doesn't want to break into my personal bubble. I kind of wish he would. I miss touch.

"You weren't there, and encouraging someone to follow their dreams doesn't mean you kil-... doesn't mean you had anything to do with their death."

"That's what the resource therapist said."

"The resource therapist was right. *Is* right. You can't tear yourself up over circumstances you didn't control. Taylor's passing was an accident."

The word "accident" explodes in my head and I can feel sadness forming deep inside me. I don't want to be sad tonight, and I don't want to depress Grayson at this dinner that's supposed to be an apology for something I don't even remember anymore. I straighten on the couch and quietly clear my throat to suppress the choking feeling. "We don't have to get into this, like you said."

"I said that for your benefit. If you feel like you need to talk, please talk. Sometimes getting thoughts out to a stranger is more helpful than with someone you know."

"Getting thoughts out to someone who isn't Caitlyn is... I don't know. It feels like my grief should be a secret? Like because it's been a year, I should be over it by now, but I'm not, not entirely. But in so many ways, I'm moving on."

"What are you feeling right now?" He sets his half-empty wine glass on the coffee table. "Not in a psychoanalyst kind of way, but about me being here?"

"I feel... honestly?"

"Of course."

I suck in a deep breath, ready for word vomit to fall from my mouth. I can't look at Grayson as I speak because if I do, I think I'll see pity in his eyes. The last thing I want is pity. "I feel like I'm betraying Taylor by having dinner with another man. I feel like everything about loving him forever is a lie if I begin to move on. I feel too many things and not enough things. I feel everything and nothing, but the things all together feel forced. Like I'm hiding. Like I'm just riding a raft until a big grief wave knocks me over."

Jovi plunks his pig on the floor next to me, emphasizing the end of what I've said. I reach for the damp toy and toss it over my shoulder down the darkening hallway before he takes off and doesn't bother coming back.

I hold my breath, waiting for a reaction.

But when I get one, it's not what I expect. "Do you want me to leave, Maggie? I won't be offended if you say you do."

Letting out a breath, I respond, rubbing a hand over my cheek. "No. I'm sorry. I don't want you to go. I just, maybe I don't understand what we're doing here."

"You don't have to be sorry. I'm not sure why we're here either. I just… I thought maybe there was a reason I kept running into you."

"Maybe it's just a frequency illusion." I shrug, and my belly rumbles. I do my best to hide the sound by continuing to speak. "We see each other around because we've met now. We see what we want to see, that sort of thing."

"Maybe it's destiny?"

"I'm not sure I believe in destiny."

"Honestly, neither am I." Grayson chuckles, picking up his wine glass from the coffee table. The way his muscles ripple under his shirt makes me feel hot around the collar of my tee, not doing anything to help with the summer heat. "Either way, Maggie, we're both here now and there's chicken parmigiana to eat. So why don't we have some dinner and we can analyze everything else once we're full?"

His gaze flicks from my face to my stomach, which growls again, and then he meets my eyes once more with that dashing smile that I'm becoming more and more familiar with.

"Yes, let's do that." I rise from the couch, unfurling my legs from their crunched-up position. "And by the way, I'm from Newfoundland, my father's name was Roger and he was a fisherman, and, well, the last question doesn't apply."

Grayson smiles, then laughs as I walk toward the kitchen to fetch the food. "Well, why'd you become a painter then?"

I don't answer right away, putting on my mitts to take the still-warm chicken from the oven. I pull the sheet pan out and set it down on the kitchen island that stands between Grayson and me. The scent of tomato and cheese wafts around us, reminding me that I haven't eaten for most of the day. " I just wanted to take colors and apply them to every day to make things brighter. Like that wall—it's the color of..."

I stop, realizing what I've almost said, and that Grayson wouldn't have any understanding of Taylor yellow and why I had to get rid of it.

"The Caribbean?" He fills in the blank, and I nod, even though the inspiration for the shade of blue on the wall is a man who is looking right back at me, and an ocean that's not all that far from my door.

"Yeah, exactly."

Chapter Nine

TAKING A PAGE FROM Grayson's earlier suggestion, we keep the conversation over dinner light while Jovi takes a nap on the sofa with his stuffed pig. The sunset sparkles over the water outside the window, a familiar cerise summer glow that I recreated once upon a time with my paints, as the fading daylight casts shadows on the wooden dining table. We chew our food thoughtfully, talking at length about everything from favorite colors to which wines we prefer. It's a little like a game, one question of mine followed by an answer of his and so forth. There's a tinge of formality to the discussion at the beginning, but as the meal starts with chicken parmigiana and leads to leftover breadcrumbs and bits of pasta, we loosen up again.

Or maybe the wine loosens us, because we're nearly through the two bottles of white by the time I stand to clear our dishes. Grayson rises as well, reaching across the table and taking my plate and silverware before I have a chance to collect his. "You sit, enjoy the rest of the wine. I'll clear this up."

"It's okay, really. I have to get the cheesecake anyway and …"

"Maggie, I'll get it. Just enjoy the sunset. Maybe it'll give you some inspiration?" Grayson picks up the rest of the dishes from the small table and carries them into the kitchen, setting them on the counter before opening the dishwasher to load them. Little does he know that my painting has been more inspired by him lately than by the beauty of the landscapes around me.

Sipping at the rest of my wine, I can't help but watch him. Grayson's careful not to clang the plates together, and the fluid motion of him standing and leaning over the large appliance seems so natural—like he knows this house and the kitchen and everything in it. Something about having him here has suddenly melted into normalcy, and I can't tell if it's because I've had too much wine or if it's his nature that makes me comfortable. Like we've known each other for a while. Kind of like with Josie, where we became friends almost instantly. Except this is the kind of friendship where I can't stop the fluttering feeling in my stomach.

A moment later, after shutting the dishwasher door, Grayson looks back at me. He catches my glance before I have an opportunity to look away. "Everything okay?"

I rip my gaze from him, staring down at the floor for a second in a vague attempt to make it appear as if I haven't been watching his every move. Watching *and* thinking. "Yeah, everything's fine. The little plates for dessert are in the top cupboard next to the stove. Forks are in the drawer on the opposite side by the fridge."

Grayson smiles before turning to collect the dishes, giving me the perfect opportunity to give him a once over from the back as well: tall, broad, handsome. Strong shoulder muscles and thick thighs, a narrow waist... wait, why am I noticing these things? Where's my head at? I can't possibly... no, *couldn't possibly* be thinking about how I'm attracted to him. It's not right. It's not a proper thought. I'm not normal for thinking about another man other than Taylor, am I? Like Caitlyn said, it's only just been a year. And a year isn't that long.

I bite the inside of my lip as Grayson pulls utensils from the drawer, crossing the kitchen to fetch the pre-sliced cake from where I'd left it to thaw on the countertop. Panic sits in my chest, banging on my ribs as he places a plate and fork in front of me. I don't think I can have anything more to eat. And I can't eat because I'm doing something wrong, aren't I? I shouldn't be here alone with Grayson, because Caitlyn said it's too soon. Even though I hate the concept of someone else deciding when and where and at what time I'm allowed to let my my life move forward, maybe she's right?

The anxiety must be written all over my face.

"Maggie, did you want a slice? I figured you'd want to pick your own piece but I can..."

"No, no," I interrupt, shaking my head and picking up my wine glass to twirl between my fingers as a distraction. "It's okay. I think I'm going to finish this wine first."

Grayson serves himself a small slice of cake before he scans me up and down, the motion of his eyes subtle, but not so subtle that I don't notice. "Something's wrong."

"No," I say again, though the word has lost its meaning and I'm certain he knows it. "Nothing's wrong. I'm just thinking. Thinking and a little tipsy. Definitely don't let me get up yet." I force out a tiny laugh before I take a sip of the sweet, now warm wine, looking out the window toward the piece of the ocean that can be seen from this angle. He's right about watching the sunset. It's stunning on this summer night.

The longer I look at it in the silence, the more the beating of my heart goes from an overactive tympanic rhythm to something that could be considered normal. But the quiet has already turned awkward by the time I finish the final sip of wine; at least, it feels uncomfortable to me. Maybe because there are too many things going on in my head and I'm over analyzing everything.

Grayson clears his throat and shuffles in his chair, standing again. Jovi lifts his head from his spot on the loveseat, probably wondering if he's going to get to go play in the yard. "I think maybe I should go."

Furrowing my brow, I nearly knock over the table as I rush to stand up as well. I'm not sure what to say, though my thoughts are suddenly going a thousand miles a minute. The alcohol rushes to my head and I nearly trip over my own feet. I grab for the edge of the table to hold me steady. It's only a second later when I blurt out the only thing I can think of, because even though I think I'm doing something wrong, everything I feel right now—confusion, excitement, interest, compassion—makes me wonder if there's also a part that's right. Maybe I'm a grief boat meeting a different kind of ship, and maybe, even though we fly different country's flags, but we're meant to go sailing together.

"I thought you said that you thought we kept running into each other for a reason?" My voice is surprisingly clear considering the amount of white wine I've consumed, well outside of my normal limit of zero drinks.

Grayson's expression is soft, but seemingly unwavering. "I thought you said it was a frequency illusion?"

"I... at least stay for dessert, Grayson. I'll do my best not to overthink or overanalyze your answers to my questions."

I'm on the verge of begging, because I don't want to be alone in this house. Even with Jovi, I'll still be left here talking to myself, and with no painting to work on and no inspiration to start something of my own, I know I'll be lonely. Maybe that's what the pain of missing someone is— the hurt of loneliness. Grayson's presence brings new colors into a world that was previously shades of muted yellow. Blue, namely. And blue is something I can live with. Blue doesn't mean shipwrecks. It means depth and water and summer and sky. Blue means calm, and when I look up into Grayson's pool blue eyes, I do my best to breathe and settle myself.

Grayson hums to himself for a moment, and I feel a bead of nervous sweat slide down the back of my neck and disappear under my tee. "How about we take the cheesecake and wine outside and sit on the patio? I think maybe being here, in the house, with all your memories…"

He doesn't finish his sentence and he doesn't have to because I know what he's going to say. The house is filled with Taylor, not physically but in memories, and maybe flooding it with the presence of another man is too much for me. Too consuming. Too small and too trapped and too conflicting.

"There's a lot of him still in here, isn't there?" I murmur, tapping my fingers on the tabletop with my eyes averted.

"A lot that you're trying to cover up. Paint over. Like that blue wall."

I look up, feeling immediately exposed. "How'd you know about the wall?"

Grayson picks up his plate of cake and pokes a fork into the top of the piece. "I didn't know, but you just told me."

Deflating, I feel the fiery heat of the sweat droplets cascade down my back and sink into my shirt hem. "It used to be yellow. Taylor's favorite color was yellow. But yellow reminds me of eggs and eggs remind me of shipwrecks and it's just, I know it doesn't make sense when I put it like that. But it does to me."

"It's okay," Grayson assures me. "It's pain, and the way we process pain doesn't always make sense."

Sucking in a deep breath, I hold it in for a few seconds before sighing it out. "You're right. It doesn't."

He offers me a gentle smile. "Come have dessert with me. Maybe that will help. Cake is like a temporary bandage."

Grayson waits patiently as I serve myself a slice of cheesecake before following him to the front door. The light is low in the house and I walk across the open space to flick on a lamp before looking down at Jovi, who is watching me expectantly. "Come on, Jovi. You might as well go outside too."

Jovi hops off the couch with his stuffed pig, and Grayson opens the door for the three of us to walk out onto the patio. As I cross the threshold between the inside and outdoors, I'm immediately hit with the scent of salt and summer and vanilla, the light breeze blowing them around me in a pirouette of aromas. Jovi trots off down the steps and out into the yard, while Grayson takes a seat on the staircase, placing his cake down on the boards. There's not much room on the steps for both of us, but it would be weird if I sat somewhere farther away, so I plunk myself down next to him on the wooden slats.

We watch Jovi run circles in the grass for a few moments, savoring the flavor of the cake and the early summer heat. I savor the company too, but I don't know if Grayson does because I'm not in his head. However, he's showing a little about how he's feeling, with his words, with his gestures, with the way he responds with his body language. Being outside doesn't seem as constricting as being in the house, and maybe it really does have something to do with the memories and the nostalgia I've tried to cover up or throw away. But the letter still exists inside, unread for the most part, and the thought of it seeps into my thoughts and my blood.

"Grayson?"

"Hmmm?" He places his fork down on the now-empty plate, and I pop my final bite of cheesecake into my mouth and swallow.

"How did you end up with the letter from Taylor?"

Grayson breathes in a deep mouthful of dusk air. "I got it in the mail."

"Someone mailed it to you? They could have just sent it to me directly, wouldn't you think? And I didn't see postage on the envelope or anything…" I scratch at the side of my cheek as I bite the skin on the inside. Something isn't sitting quite right. "How would anyone get hold of something of Taylor's and not know to send it to me or Caitlyn?"

"It was mailed before anyone would have been gathering up his possessions, I presume. I mean, based on the postal date on the original envelope."

"Wait, there was another envelope with this envelope inside of it? What else was in there?" My heart is starting to race again, and I can't tell if it's because I'm anxious or if it's the alcohol or something else entirely.

Grayson hesitates for a few seconds, and I try to pry into his head with my gaze. The time ticks away, feeling like hours, and Jovi scrambles between us to collect a driftwood stick before running back out into the yard. "I got a letter too. Nothing like I imagine yours is. Basically, just instructions saying to give the envelope to you if anything ever happened."

My insides feel all mixed up, like the chicken parmigiana isn't sitting well in combination with the sweet wine. " I need more information."

"I... how do I put this? Taylor was a friend. One of those people you connect with right away. I know he wasn't in the Navy very long before last summer when he got posted here, but we became work buddies, you know? He hadn't connected with many of the other guys yet, but he was really worried about going back out to sea and leaving you here. I think one of the guys talked about him and his wife putting together a will and it kind of freaked him out." Grayson runs a hand over his cropped hair, rubbing the back of his neck.

I crinkle my forehead, trying to put the pieces together. "Taylor never talked about that sort of thing. He was more the silent type when it came to his concerns but... I should have thought about that after he went to sea the first time and couldn't tell me where he was. I felt so lost."

"It doesn't make most of us happy, but it's safer that way." He adjusts his position on the steps, the stars beginning to twinkle over his head as Jovi flops down in the grass by our feet with his discarded stuffed pig. "He talked about you a lot. You meant everything to him. I think he didn't want to worry you more than he knew you were already worried."

I nod, blinking up at the fading daylight for a minute, trying to absorb the magnitude of what he's saying. Grayson and Taylor were friends, even though I'd never heard his name mentioned. Taylor was more private than I am, but I didn't expect he was withholding as much information from me as it seems like he was. "So, the timing of all this was just random? How come you held on to the letter for so long?"

"I didn't," Grayson notes with a bit of a shrug. "It must have gotten lost in the mail because it only showed up in my mailbox the day before I brought it to you. Original date of processing still stamped on it and everything. I don't know why he didn't just hand it to me and ask me to hold onto it, but if I had to take a guess, knowing him, he wouldn't have wanted to make it a public request."

It would be exactly like Taylor to mail a letter rather than ask someone outright to help him—an old-fashioned action for a modern-day request. Something about it feels romantic, like our Saturday breakfasts in bed. But I never took Taylor for a love letter kind of person, and I certainly didn't know he connected with Grayson.

"Do you think it would help you to read my letter from Taylor?" Grayson asks, his voice low. "I can bring it with me the next time we meet?"

I shake my head. "It's okay. I know that the words in my letter are precious and personal, and I'm sure you must feel the same way about what he said to you. Taylor meant those things for you, and you alone. I don't think it would be right for me to read them."

We sit on the patio with our empty plates next to us for another few moments, the distant waves on the shoreline rocks a quiet symphony. As we sit, night rolls in, soft and gentle and dark, the solar lights in the front garden lighting up with a dim glow that rivals the moonlit bloom of the evening sky. The temperature drops with the setting of the sun, and soon my T-shirt and shorts aren't nearly enough to keep me warm. Goosebumps begin to form on my arms and legs, and soon I find myself shivering. However, despite the chill, I don't particularly want to leave the warm atmosphere that surrounds Grayson to run in and grab a sweater and put on some leggings. Maybe it's an effect of the alcohol but my insides feel warm, though my outside does not.

Grayson notices. "Maggie, you're shivering."

"It's a little cold." I shrug nonchalantly, not sure why I'm trying to hide that I'm going to need more clothing if we stick around on the patio for much longer.

"I'd say we could go sit inside so you don't freeze, but..." He coughs, leaning against the banister of the porch.

I bite the corner of my lip, understanding what he's saying but not sure what to do about it. I'd like to have him in the house, but there are so many memories I'm trying to manage that I don't know if the hours that have passed are enough to have counteracted my apprehension and nostalgia. "Yeah. It got dark fast. Maybe I should go change."

"What time is it, anyway?" Grayson pulls his phone from his pocket, the screen lighting up his face as he presses a button on the side. He makes a little humming noise and taps the screen so it goes black again. "I should head home. Perdita probably needs to go outside."

"Oh, no problem." I reach over for his empty plate, stacking it on top of mine and topping it with our dirty forks. We both rise from our seated positions on the porch steps and I set the plates on the wide railing, Grayson standing a quarter of the way down the stairs while I'm on the top landing. I don't want to hold him up if he really does need to leave. "Thanks for having dinner with me. I'm sorry if it was—if I was… well, I hope it wasn't too strange for you. I appreciated the company. It's been a long time since I've had someone around to have a conversation with over my chicken parmigiana."

The corner of Grayson's lips twitches upward. "Not strange at all, Maggie. Thanks for inviting me."

We stand there for a moment, the seconds ticking by because neither of us seems to know what to do next. As he looks me over with his blue eyes, I'm trying desperately to avoid them because they're making my stomach do cartwheels. But as hard as I try not to look in his direction, my heart is begging for me to give in and meet his glance. Give in and allow myself to feel the way I'm feeling without being guilty over what Caitlyn said about a year not being all that long.

But what is it that I'm feeling? It can't be anything that I've felt before with Taylor because that wouldn't be right. But everything about the way Grayson looks and looks at me makes me all twisted on the inside—in a good way. In a way that makes my mouth dry and my palms sweat with the idea of… no, I can't be thinking about kissing him?

I haven't been lonely for nearly long enough to justify kissing another man, even if the man does have the bluest, kindest eyes I've ever seen.

"Is everything okay?" Grayson furrows his brow and it strikes me that I've been standing here looking up and down and all around without saying a proper goodbye. Even Jovi's staring at me from the bottom step, waiting for me to tell him to get into the house before the bugs start to gather around the porch light.

"Everything's fine." The words come out a little bit shaky, but I end the statement as strongly as I possibly can. "I'm just thinking. Was just thinking. Hoping, I guess, that we'd run into each other again some time."

The words fall out of my mouth before I'm able to stop myself from saying them. They feel so forward, like I'm asking for the world, but Grayson just smiles and lets out a little chuckle.

"Honestly, I was hoping that we might too. Maybe on purpose next time."

I grin as Jovi trots up the stairs to find a spot by my side. "Wasn't this on purpose?"

"It was. But I'd like to do it again too if you're comfortable with it."

Am I? I'm still in shock that Grayson's willing to meet up with me again after I acted the way I did tonight, after being strange about being in the house, after showing him the studio and talking about Taylor probably more than

I should have. Am I comfortable with it? Should I be as comfortable with it as my mind is telling me I am? What about what Caitlyn said?

I shove the memory of my conversation with Caitlyn out of my mind. "Of course. I'd like it. Like to meet up again, I mean."

"Should I text you?" Grayson pulls out his phone again. "I can send you those photos from the other day at the beach to see if there's anything you'd want to paint. Or email? Do you have a preference?"

"Maybe text? I can always send the photos to my computer later. I'm 555-9375."

He taps away on the device, a brilliant yellow glow lighting up his face as his large fingers type in what I presume is my name and number. As I stand there, starting to shiver again, I realize that I'm clammy all over; excited and nervous and chilly put together in one body that can't believe I have just given my phone number to a man for the first time since I can remember.

Grayson pockets the phone. "Got it. I'll text you the photos when I get home after I let Perdi out."

"Sounds good to me." I nod, feeling more goosebumps rise on my arms despite the fact that I didn't think that was possible.

"Good night, Maggie."

I finally allow myself to meet his eyes for longer than half a second, the lamplight glowing on Grayson's face. What would happen if I stepped down the stairs? What if I... no. I don't care what Taylor's note said about letting him go, because it's Caitlyn's words that echo in my head and my heart as I reply, "Good night, Grayson."

He slowly turns and descends the stairs to the front walkway, heading toward the hatchback in the drive. I stay out on the porch until his headlights back down to the road and fade away, even though I don't know why I bother because I don't think he can see me standing here with Jovi next to me. Either way, I escape back into the house, away from the blackflies. As I close the front door and lock it, a smile breaks over my face and I realize that it's been a long time since I've felt the way I'm feeling. And maybe I know more about the way that I'm feeling than I'd like to admit.

Scratching at a rising bug bite on my neck, I flick off the lights to the living room and call Jovi to come to bed. We head down the hallway, his claws clicking on the floor before he steps onto the bedroom rug. Digging out a pair of pants and a new T-shirt, I put on the warmer clothes before crawling under the blankets, the husky hopping into his usual spot that used to be Taylor's. The scent of the ocean has permeated the space, and I leave the window open despite that chill I was trying to avoid.

I have my eyes closed, trying to sleep amid the sound of the sea, when a small gust blows and flutters Taylor's letter to the floor. With a sigh, I hoist myself up and reach over the edge of the bed to fetch the sheets of paper. I don't want to read them, and yet, I do, and destiny or fate or something of the sort must want me to as well because the only page that's face-up is page two. Setting the other two pieces of notepaper on the nightstand under a small jewelry box that Taylor brought back from overseas, I squish myself up against the headboard by Jovi and prepare myself for more words that might break my heart.

The handwriting on the second page looks more rushed, the letters and words slightly running together. Taylor's blockish style is still prominent, but it appears he may have been getting carried away in what he wanted to say by the time he got to this point.

I can only hope that my last words to you were ones that you'll remember forever. And I mean that in a good way, not a bad one. I mean it in the way that I want you to know that I loved you as much as my heart could give, and then maybe even more than that. I loved you through the whole Earth, through to the moon, over the entire universe. You were more than my world, Maggie. You were my everything.

A tear prickles the corner of one eye, but I will for it to stay in because I don't want to cry. Not tonight, not after such a good day—well, minus the call from Caitlyn. If I don't want to cry, I shouldn't be reading this following page of Taylor's letter, but now that I've started, I can't let go.

But even despite being everything, I can't be everything to you always. As I said, Mags—please miss me, but let me go. I want you to smile again. I want you to move on. And I want you to know that even if I'm somewhere up in the stars watching down on you to make sure you stay safe, it will make me and my spirit and my soul happy to know that you are happy too.

Tracing my finger across the page, I can clearly feel the indentations of the pen he used to write the words. He wants me to be happy, but I don't know if I can be happy without him. But then again, I was happy today, wasn't I? I was happy with Grayson. Is that the kind of happiness that Taylor means?

Jovi sighs next to me, and I absently reach over to pat his head with my free hand.

I'm going to ask my close colleague Grayson Smith to deliver this letter. I found his address in our files from the clerk's office. I trust that he'll get it to you safely. I trust that he'll know the reason behind you needing it, and I hope that my words and his presence bring you some comfort and some closure. There's nothing you could have done to make this end any different, Maggie. This was my dream, and I appreciate every second of you supporting it.

The page stops there, and so do I.

With the first page of Taylor's letter, I was left with a million questions. With this second page, my heart is getting ripped from my chest. The image of Taylor being a star watching down on me breaks my own soul into pieces, shattering it like the moon's reflection on broken glass. It hurts even more because of all the pinpricks of light that are outside the bedroom window. Taylor's keeping me safe, and maybe watching me read the words he wrote a year ago and wondering why it's taken so long. Does he know about the post office mix-up? Does he know that I can't stop thinking about Grayson? What are the odds that

I'd start to develop feelings for the very man who brought me this love letter from my late husband?

I'm in the middle of beginning to panic when my phone dings from its spot on the bedside table. I must jump half a foot in the air because Jovi startles from the other side of the comforter.

Unknown: Hi, Maggie. It's Grayson. Just realized I didn't give you my number in case you happened to want to contact me. Thanks again for supper, it was nice to see you again. (7 attachments)

Before I reply, I click the icons to load the large graphics on my phone. It only takes a minute, but soon, gorgeous gray skies and a rough ocean appear on my screen, along with the off-brown of the sandy beach, white gulls, and stormy smoke of the boulders. Every one of the seven pictures he's attached is atmospheric and ethereal, like they were taken on a planet other than our own. Like he sees the world through his camera lens in a way that I never expected him to. Like I'm seeing him in a way I never expected to. As more than pretty blue eyes and a kind smile and gentle soul. As someone who is opening up that broken heart-shaped box in my chest.

Maggie: These are amazing.

Grayson: They're nothing much. Just quick shots from the other day when we ran into you.

I think about all the colors and shades mixed together, some of them sitting in my studio in tubes with names like "sea smoke" and "midnight blue" and how I'm going to make them into the right hues for every one of these photographs. How I might not be able to wait until the morning. How these photos are representative of Taylor and Grayson and my feelings all at the same time.

Maggie: They're beautiful. Seriously. I'm not sure I can wait to print them off and get started.

Grayson: If you do, I'd love to buy one.

Maggie: No charge. They're your photos. But I'll definitely be using them if that's okay with you? I'll credit you on the website and we can work out a portion of the cost or I can pay you however you want to be paid.

Grayson: It's fine, Maggie. Seeing them painted and you inspired by them is enough for me.

Grayson: Also, I wanted to ask... there's an art exhibit happening tomorrow evening on the waterfront. Would you have any interest in joining me to have a look around?

My face flushes with heat for a moment before I type a message back, sinking deep into the pillows that smell like the ocean, a fresh breeze, and a bit of dried paint. Another night with Grayson sounds like just the thing I need, and who can argue with a starlit night combined with art?

Maggie: Absolutely.

Grayson responds with a little smiling face emoji before a second message pops up on my phone screen.

Grayson: Want me to pick you up? Easier to find parking for one car than two.

He definitely has a point, though I feel a bit apprehensive at the idea of sitting in a car so close to him, even though it will only be for a short period.

Maggie, you have to get over your fears. Your guilt. Your grief.

And so, I type out another short message, going against the anxious thoughts in my head.

Maggie: That would be great. What time?

Grayson: I'll see you at nine. Have a good rest of your night.

Maggie: Thanks, Grayson. You too.

Chapter Ten

The day passes by slowly, despite the fact that I'd like for it to pass more quickly in order to get to nine o'clock when Grayson will arrive. I spend the day with Jovi playing in the yard, cleaning up some of the overgrown plants in the garden that have taken root in the grass. By the time I'm done, it's past suppertime, and I feed Jovi and heat up a little something for myself. After that, my stomach is doing cartwheels and I almost wish I hadn't eaten anything. I draw myself a bath to clean up and try to relax a little before the art exhibit.

I'm not sure if the water relaxes me, despite the bubbles and the soothing temperature. I dig under my fingernails to remove every speck of dirt, every remnant of paint, every iota of the afternoon. I try to lean back against the bath pillow that Taylor bought for me one Christmas and think about something calming and soothing, but all my head and my heart want to consider is the blue of Grayson's eyes and the guilty pang in my chest I get when I think about him.

I relax for about three seconds, which might be a record for me outside of the complete distraction that comes with painting.

Half an hour later, I'm ready for Grayson's arrival, but it's still a bit early, so I find myself puttering around the kitchen, tidying up the countertops and wiping down the cupboards just for something to do. The feeling of anxiety is palpable, but there's nothing I can figure out to do that will make it go away.

Other than wait for Grayson's little black hatchback to arrive in my driveway.

Which it does, moments before nine o'clock.

The sun has disappeared into the dark, with little speckles of stars overhead that look like flickers of paint in the canvas of midnight blue. I'm just slipping on a pair of comfortable flats when there's a tiny knock at the door, a shadowy shape of a man on the other side holding something in his left hand. Jovi runs down the hallway from where he was napping on my bed, barking his fool head off.

I slide one foot into a shoe and open the door to face Grayson, who is holding a small flower in a blue pot. He's wearing a pair of chinos and a collared shirt, along with a broad smile that is so contagious I find myself grinning back as I hold Jovi by the collar so he doesn't run into the yard.

Grayson reaches out his hand a bit, showing off the plant. "Brought you a little something. Supposed to be easy to take care of. At least, that's what the woman at House 'N Home said. I didn't want to make your life more complicated, but..." Grayson trails off, his smile wavering just a touch, before he turns the conversation in a different direction. "Anyway, I was thinking a kitchen window might be nice."

"I think you're right. Jovi, sit down." Miraculously, Jovi listens to me, and I take the flower from Grayson, looking down at the violet petals in their sky-blue container. I'm careful not to touch him as I do so, because I'm not sure what I'd feel if our fingers were to brush right now. Though admittedly I'm not sure what to do right at the moment, holding Jovi in one hand and the plant in the other, looking up at Grayson and grinning.

It's sweet that he brought me a little gift, and I can't help but wonder if Josie might have been the person to help him pick it out since he said he bought it at House 'N Home.

"Here, let me hold onto Jovi while you put that somewhere he can't get into it. Then we can get going?"

Nodding, I wait for Grayson's hand to run along the dog's collar before I let go, making certain for a second time that we don't accidentally touch. When Jovi's secure and Grayson's scratching him behind the ears, I stride over to the kitchen and place the pretty flower on the window ledge, listening to Grayson talk to Jovi.

"Where's your toys? You gonna be good while mom's gone and play by yourself?"

"Ah," I say, walking back. "You said the magic word. Other than 'b-e-a-c-h.'"

"Which one?"

"Toy. If you let him go, I suspect he'll hunt down his squeaky pig. Go on, Jovi. Go get your pig toy and go to bed."

Grayson tentatively releases Jovi's collar, and the husky takes off down the hallway back toward the bedroom. "Guess that means you're ready to leave?"

I pick up my wristlet from the side table next to the door and then meet Grayson's gentle gaze. My earlier anxiety about tonight melts away, like it's an ice cube out in the warm sun. It doesn't disappear all at once, but a little at a time. "Sure."

Grayson steps down off the front patio and waits for me to lock the door. Once I've clipped my keys to the ring of my wrist-wallet, Grayson's standing by the passenger's side of his hatchback, door open and waiting for me to take my seat.

I can't help but laugh. "You don't have to hold doors open for me, you know. I can get into the car on my own."

His lip twitches upward in an even more prominent smile, showing off a dimple in his cheek, but not saying anything. Just waiting—for me.

I cross the front lawn and take a seat in the black car, the heat of the day contrasted with the coolness of the interior air conditioning that must have been blasting all the way over here. Grayson shuts the door, never losing that boyish grin, and crosses around to the front of the car with his keys dangling off one finger in the partial darkness. There's no helping the way I watch him as he moves, his thighs pressing against the fabric of his pants, the muscles of his arms stretching against the sleeves of his shirt. He's not hard to look at, that's for certain, but the moment I allow myself to accept that thought, the guilt sets in.

Maybe I'm doing something wrong.

Grayson opens the door and takes his own seat, twisting the key in the car's ignition and allowing the engine to come to life. Headlights glow against the siding of my house, and soon we're backing out of the driveway and driving toward downtown.

The thing I notice first as we turn the corner at the end of my road onto the main street next to the beach is that I can smell the scent of Grayson's shampoo, cologne, something—mixed with the subtle scent of a car air freshener in a pine aroma. It's masculine but faint, reminiscent of the woods and peppermint and a bonfire, sitting in my nostrils and making me feel something I haven't felt in a long, long time.

I next thing I notice nearly cancels out the sensations: the two of us are close, here, in the car. One of Grayson's hands rests on the gear shift, the other hand on the bottom of the steering wheel, while he leans back in a relaxed posture. I can't imagine that I look that relaxed, sitting straight up in the passenger's seat, my wristlet on my lap, hands tightly coiled together as I'm biting my lip. Once I'm aware I'm doing all of these things, I let out a breath that's more of a sigh.

It's okay, Maggie. This is okay.

Grayson and I make small talk across the bridge, the radio playing something low in the background. Things are light—airy, even—despite my awkwardness and crushing anxiety. I can't help but feel things from being so close to Grayson, but as I talk, I attempt to envision pushing those feelings away as well so they don't affect me too much. Once the conversation turns to talking about the dogs, I'm able to rattle off story after story about Jovi and our little adventures out of the house. The tales last until we pull into the parking garage downtown, Grayson turning off the engine to the hatchback and smiling at me from the driver's seat.

"Have you ever been to Nocturne before?"

I shake my head. "I don't think I've ever heard of it until now. I'm kind of excited to see what it's all about."

"I hope you'll enjoy it. There's a lot of walking, but the sore feet will be worth it, I think."

I grin back at Grayson, who practically looks through my soul with his clear, blue eyes before he exits the car and I follow suit. It takes a moment before I realize that my hands are shaking, my nerves getting the best of me. However, as we take the stairs out of the parking garage at Purdy's Wharf and stroll toward the waterfront boardwalk, I start to relax under the darkness and the starlight. Maybe it's because Grayson can't see my anxiety under the moon—or at least I hope he isn't able to *feel* it.

We walk along the coastline for a few minutes before we come to the first exhibit: light art cast on the side of the seaside hotel, moving to the sounds of acoustic music playing into the night. It's quite pretty watching the array of colors form scenes that accent the selection of tracks playing: pale blues and rich reds and hunter greens melting with burning oranges that flash delicately into the evening. There's a billboard posted with information about the installation, and Grayson and I peek over the writing in silence, reading to ourselves under a small lamp.

"It's neat, isn't it?" Grayson finally breaks the silence between us, though the atmosphere certainly isn't quiet. "The way the patterns seem to move with the beat of the music? I've always wondered how things like this work."

I think about attempting to explain the magic behind the art to him, but as soon as I open my mouth to do so, I clamp it quickly shut again. Perhaps part of enjoying the installation is not knowing how every aspect of it works, and just enjoying it for what it is instead of the process behind creating it. Especially since it isn't my art to explain.

We watch the light show until the end of the next song, standing around and trying to stay out of the way of the growing crowds. When the music fades and a new track begins, I peer over at Grayson, then past him, looking around at the next group of people on the wharf. Standing tall above them are lamp posts, but they aren't lights in the traditional sense. They look as if they've been melted down in the summer heat, starting to collapse from the clay that's formed them.

"That's kind of interesting," I say, gazing over toward the next exhibit with my head tilted ever so slightly to the side. "I wonder how long it took to make that."

Grayson turns around and looks toward the wharf. "Maybe the sign will say something about the process. Want to go have a look?"

I nod and lead the two of us over to the pier's edge where the large lampposts are situated. People are milling about taking pictures with the post that's "melted" almost completely to the wharf's wooden planks, while Grayson and I stand under one that's tall and curved in the middle. The lights on the posts are bright and functional, though there's still a little book light by the podium with information on the installation.

Grayson casts his gaze over the laminated paper, giving me time to stare up into the starry night and lamplit blue before he speaks. "Doesn't say anything other than 'months to create.' I wonder how they even managed to move it here. Fascinating, really."

"I used to always find other people's art so inspiring. It's been hard since—"

He smiles, seemingly knowing that I don't want to talk about the shipwreck but it always finds its way to the tip of my tongue no matter what. "I'm sure it has."

We stand there amid the buzz of the waterfront for a few moments, neither of us saying anything, my heart beating against my ribcage. It's almost as if it's trying to tell me something, but I can't translate what the message is because I've been repressing so many feelings for the last year. Something in my twitchy fingers wants me to reach over and hold Grayson's hand—to try and find some stability in this unstable world—but I don't, and he doesn't either because he's probably not thinking the same thing as me.

"Want to keep walking?" I finally say, hoping that my suddenness doesn't come across as disinterest in the exhibits. Thankfully, Grayson seems to take my suggestion with a single nod.

We follow along the waterfront's worn wooden boards for some time, taking in multiple other installations and acts. There are some physical art pieces on stands, large sculptures in front of buildings, and colorful displays of all different types underneath the moonlit eve. It takes us about an hour and a bit to walk through the entire loop of, stopping at the final installation which is a collection of life-size porcelain rabbits perched in long grass on the side of a small gradient. The little bunny family has me thinking, looking, wanting to touch the art even though I know better than to reach my hand out and alter the position of the ceramic pieces. It's beautiful in the simplicity of it all, three tiny babies next to a mother and father rabbit, curled like little balls underneath an overgrown plant that just so happens to be in exactly the right location.

"This one's called 'Family,'" Grayson notes. "We probably wouldn't have even noticed it if there wasn't a sign. It's sort of hidden."

"That's part of the beauty and meaning of the installation, I think. We don't always notice something when it's right in front of us."

Grayson's lips twitch in a small knowing smile, but he doesn't respond. Instead, he waits patiently while I snap a couple of photos of the almost-hidden rabbits with my phone. My ankles crack as I stand from my crouched position next to the grass, pocketing the device with a satisfied grin—satisfied that we found part of the exhibit that others might have missed.

"Where to now?" I ask.

"You hungry at all? I was thinking we could get a pastry and make this the whole downtown experience. But judging by the crowd over by Beavertails, we might have to eat in the car."

"It might be nice to get a little bit of quiet anyway. Let's grab something for the road."

Grayson and I nearly bump shoulders as we start walking toward the Beavertails shack, but I force myself to shift away from him even though I can't help but wonder what it would feel like if we touched. I'm so preoccupied with the thought that I barely manage to make my pastry order: chocolate and cinnamon. Grayson orders a plain with cinnamon, pays for the both of us, and the teen working at the late-night stand places our orders in brown bags before handing them over and beckoning to the next people in line.

"You really didn't have to pay for mine," I note as we walk away, heading back toward the parking garage.

"You didn't have to come out with me tonight. It's my treat."

I consider telling him that I wanted more than anything to see him again, but my heart tells me that I should feel guilty about the sentiment instead of proud of it, so I don't say anything other than to provide Grayson with a quick thank you. When we get back to the car, up the stairs to the sixth level of the tower, he holds the passenger's door open for me again before getting in his own side of the car, buckling himself in, and turning on the air conditioning.

"I don't want to make a mess in your car..." I start to say, but Grayson flicks his hand.

"Please, Maggie. Perdi makes enough of a mess in here with all her fur. You're probably going to accidentally take home a whole new dog on your clothes. Don't worry about a little cinnamon sugar."

We pull our pastries out of their bags and quietly munch away, the bright incandescent lights of the parking tower casting a harsh glow over the car. After a few bites and half a song on the radio, Grayson clears his throat. "This isn't really the way I wanted to end the night. Would you be good to eat while I drive back to the Port? At least over there we can see the stars."

My mouth half full of warm chocolate and sprinkled cinnamon, I nod. Moments later, we're heading out of the waterfront parking garage and onto the ramp for the bridge to the other side of the peninsula, Grayson's half-eaten Beavertail on his lap for him to pick at once we get out of the city.

I munch away on my pastry the whole way back to Eastern Port, Grayson and I talking quietly about the exhibit over the acoustic songs on the radio. My favorite installation was definitely the rabbits, and I feel a sensation of tightness in my chest when I talk about the way they affected me—though I can't quite put a finger on the reason for why. It might have something to do with the little hidden family in the grass, the idea that the porcelain animals have a family when I feel as if I do not, Caitlyn being the only person I have left who is remotely close to a relative.

Before I know it, Grayson's pulling his hatchback into my driveway, and the night is coming to a close. I feel as if I dominated the conversation the whole way home with my feelings about ceramic bunnies, and so I decide it is probably time for me to take myself and my trauma back in the house to be alone. Again.

However, Grayson doesn't seem to be negatively affected by my blabbering, and once he turns off the car engine again, he shifts his weight in the driver's seat to look at me in the moonglow and the glimmer of the ivory porch light. Rubbing a finger over my lip, trying to remove any remnants of cinnamon and chocolate from the Beavertail, I brush my mouth before I offer up a smile. "Thanks for tonight, by the way. It was nice to be out of the house and go somewhere a little... different."

"I thought you might like the art. Every year Nocturne seems to just get better and better. I try not to miss it if I know I'm going to be on leave at the time. Last year, work got in the way." Grayson picks a crumb or a dog hair from the front of his chinos and flicks it onto the floor.

"Yeah, must be tough having that kind of a schedule."

"You'd know just as well as I do. Taylor did the same sort of thing for the time he was in service." The conversation turning to Taylor feels so natural, yet his name causes a little twinge of pain in my heart. "Sorry, I shouldn't be bringing him up, maybe..."

"It's okay. Actually, I've been curious to know more about your relationship with him. If it's not too weird and too late to be asking that." I accent the request with a little shrug to signify it's no big deal, biting the inside of my lip again in hopes that I'm not being strange by asking Grayson this. I might be trying to show it's not a big deal, but my shaking hands tell me that it is.

"Are you sure, Maggie? I don't want to make you upset or uncomfortable."

"I'm sure."

Grayson sucks in a breath before looking out the windshield toward my house. "Taylor and I were in basic training together years ago. We kind of became friends there, but nothing too serious since you never know who you're going to see again and who might be shipped off across the country. We had a few laughs, a few nights out, but he talked about you a lot. I remember that. I remember sometimes the guys and I would ask him to come out for drinks with us and he'd be on the phone with you and tell us he'd meet up later. Sometimes he did and sometimes he didn't. It wasn't personal, it was just a Taylor thing."

A little smile cracks across Grayson's face as he seemingly thinks back to his time in training, and I try to figure out where the story is going.

"Anyway, I remember one night I had a forty to myself and I was just an absolute wreck. Long story short, Taylor walked from camp to the party we were at to get my car keys and drive me and the guys back to base. That was the moment I knew he wasn't a disaster kid like the rest of us—he had plans. Real plans, Maggie. No wonder he didn't want to come out with us after that." Grayson chuckles, flicking his gaze over to me. I presume he's trying to get a read on how I'm feeling, but for some reason, the story doesn't change anything in my heart.

He must be able to sense something isn't quite right. "I'm so sorry, Maggie."

"It's… I want to say it's okay, but it's not. I feel…"

"Guilty?"

I nod again, casting my glance away from Grayson because I think I might start crying. It's everything, everything from the porcelain rabbits to the story to the Beavertail and the way we are so close here in the car. "Is that bad?"

I expect the world to end right here and right now, but Grayson shakes his head. "I don't think so. But maybe it does mean that we need more time."

"Maybe I should go."

"We're going to be saying this a lot, aren't we?"

He taps his fingers on the steering wheel, playing out an unsteady, offbeat rhythm that feels like it doesn't belong. Meanwhile, the cinnamon and pine scent of the car surrounds us both, and I'm left nostalgic for the hours before we started having this conversation.

Letting out a little puff of air, I shift positions in my seat. "Maybe we're *both* feeling guilty." I reach over toward Grayson's hand, then stop myself and retract it back to my side of the car. "Or maybe we're both feeling *something*."

Grayson under the starlight and in the glow of the moon is a beautiful thing, so beautiful that my mind begins to move more quickly than I'd like it to. I'm having thoughts I shouldn't be having, coupled with fault and shame. I can't give in to those feelings, and I can't give in to my grief ship ones, but the two are like opposing waves, making a current that batters my figurative boat and topples it around in the sea.

I should go.

"Maggie?" Grayson finally stops his tapping and looks over at me. "I hope we can do this again soon."

I gather my wristlet and my Beavertails trash, using the opportunity to leave with a minimal amount of awkwardness. Pushing open the passenger's side door on my own, I smile at Grayson as the overhead light blares on and crushes any semblance of ambiance we had created. However, his words echo in my ears, and the idea of sitting this close to Grayson again appeals to me. Therefore, I allow myself to respond, my bare arm barely brushing his as I finally remember to unbuckle my seatbelt.

"I'd like that."

Chapter Eleven

The next morning before I take Jovi out, I check the tracking numbers from the receipts on the fridge. Once I type in the long codes into the text box, I find that both Cordelia Martin and Wilhelmina Dare's paintings have arrived at their destinations. I can't help but wonder what their faces looked like when they opened up their packages with their custom work. It's the one thing I don't particularly like about my business being almost entirely on the internet—I miss some of the gratifying moments of selling my artwork, including that warm and fuzzy feeling when someone's face lights up as they open an envelope with their photograph and my replication of it inside.

Even though I try to distract myself with thoughts of happiness and good reviews on my online portal, I still can't stop thinking about the latest page in Taylor's letter and the art exhibit with Grayson yesterday evening. The two conflict with each other in my head, despite the letter telling me that Taylor wants me to be happy. I was happy with Grayson, though a bit nervous about my own feelings, but would Taylor really think that the man he sent to deliver an envelope to me would be the one I'd start to fall for in his absence?

Though it's not really an absence, per se. I mean, it is and it isn't, all at the same time. It's a permanent absence—a void, an emptiness, a nothing. It's not as if Taylor is going to return and be upset with me. I just wonder if his spirit will be unsettled if I admit to myself that I'm having romantic thoughts about Grayson.

With a sigh, I close the browser on the computer and look around at the sunny morning light streaming through the studio windows. Jovi's got another stuffed animal in his mouth, and it's making a faint, dying, squeaking noise every time he chews it.

"You ready to go to the beach?" I look over at him and he immediately drops the toy and gives me a single bark in response before trotting out of the room. He's doesn't need to be asked twice if he wants to go play outside or jump in the water.

I make my way to the front of the house, stuffing my phone in my back pocket on the way. My long-forgotten teacup sits on the edge of the kitchen island, still steaming hot and not ready for me to drink yet anyway. Sliding it away from the edge as I pass by, Jovi dances a little dog-tempo around my feet until I get close enough to the front door to satisfy his excitement. I slip on my sneakers before clipping on his leash, and soon we are making our way down over the hill and across the road to the place where the water and the rocks and the sky all meet together.

We're just crossing the faded double-yellow line on the middle of the road when I look up and spot a familiar black hatchback pull away from the edge of the street and onto the shoulder to park.

I pause, standing on the edge of the rocks and dunes, waiting for Grayson and Perdita to exit the car. Jovi waits as well, wiggling his tail back and forth next to me, thumping against my leg in time with the beating of my heart. I know what that rapid beating means now—that I'm happy to see Grayson, and that I have butterflies in my stomach when I'm around him. And maybe, based on the two pages I've read from Taylor's letter and the passage of time, that's okay.

At least, if I ignore what Caitlyn said.

My phone dings from my pocket, and I quickly check the message before tapping a response.

Josie: Morning! How have things been going?

Maggie: I'm at the beach with Jovi right now and Grayson just pulled up with his dog. Hopefully things won't be too awkward.

Josie: I won't interrupt. But just... be careful, okay? I know moving forward is important after loss, but I don't want to see you end up getting hurt with something that's happening so fast.

Maggie: Thanks, Josie. I'm taking things as slow as I can. I don't think I could manage otherwise. It's just different, you know? When you meet someone who you connect with? Anyway, I'll text you in a bit.

I tuck the device back in my pocket just as Grayson and Perdita walk up, Jovi pulling on his leash in excitement to sniff at the other dog.

"Hey, good morning." Grayson smiles at me with a wide grin that shows a shallow dimple on his cheek. Maybe it's just a trick of the light, but I swear his eyes are sparkling like the ocean. "Funny meeting you here."

Laughing, I loosen my grip on Jovi's lead and let him head toward Perdita, who looks more than happy to see him as well. "As if you didn't know I'd be here around this time."

"I might have gotten up a little early to bring Perdi for a walk."

We stand there between the road and the beach, amid the sound of the lapping waves and the occasional breeze. It's almost as if we don't know what to say past a general greeting. I want to talk about last night and make sure that I wasn't too strange, but I also don't want to seem odd for replaying the entire night. I try my hardest to think of something to say that isn't related to our outing.

"Thanks again for sending me those photographs. They're really something."

Come on, Maggie, that's the best you can do?

Grayson doesn't seem to mind my inability to make interesting conversation, or the fact that I called his artwork "something."

"Oh, it was no problem at all. I'm just glad you liked them." He bobs his shoulders up and down before looking down at Perdi and Jovi as if he's a bit embarrassed that I've brought up his photos in person. Maybe he's shy about his skills?

I look at him carefully, trying not to be noticed before he switches his gaze from the dogs to me. "You didn't bring your camera today?"

"It's in the car. I usually have it around just in case. I can go get it?"

I nod, then shake my head, then shrug. "If you want. Sometimes it's nice to just enjoy the scenery, you know?"

The corners of his lips twitch as our eyes meet. "Yeah," he replies. "I know what you mean."

My cheeks bristle with heat, and I quickly turn away toward the ocean. There aren't any ships out there this morning, probably all docked away in the yard until the local crews are assigned to go to sea again. Only gulls and the occasional tern are visible, and what looks like possibly a seal's head bobbing over the waves for a moment until it dips below the water and disappears.

"I'm going to let Jovi run. Is Perdi okay off leash? There doesn't seem to be anyone else around." I reach down and unclip the lead from the husky's collar, feet sinking in the sandy hills.

Grayson nods. "She's fine. They'll finally get to play together."

He unfastens her leash and the moment they're free, the two dogs take off over the dune's edge, down over the boulders, jumping and bouncing off each other. Jovi launches himself toward the ocean, crashing into the lapping waves with vigor, and Perdita follows close behind as the two bark and chase one another through the salty water. I can't help the grin that spreads over my face, nor the laugh that escapes me, and when I peek over at Grayson, he has a smile on his face as well.

"I guess they like each other?" I coil Jovi's leash around my hand.

"Guess so. Want to take a walk?"

"Sure, I'll follow you down."

We carefully step over the dunes, the sand slipping underneath our shoes, causing us to slide an inch or so with every step. As we make it to the boulders, Grayson hops off the large rocks, landing on the beach, reaching a hand up to help me down. I'm sure he knows that I don't actually need the assistance, but the gesture is kind and seems natural. Even still, I hesitate to take his hand in mine because it feels like the first step to admitting my feelings for him are growing into emotions that I'm struggling to be ready for, even with Taylor's message that I should allow myself to experience happiness with another person.

Almost in slow-motion, I reach my hand out and my fingers connect with Grayson's palm. There's a fleeting sensation of skin on skin, and then a soft crackle in the back of my neck like fireworks are going off in my brain and shooting sparks down my spine. He closes his fingers over mine, encasing my hand in his, and we stand there on the edge of the beach for a second or more, both looking at where we've connected and my wedding band that twinkles just enough to draw attention. His grasp is warm and I begin to feel a revelation in my heart and not just in my head—I can miss Taylor and still allow myself to move on. I can miss him but let him go. I can be happy, even if it's "only been a year." Grief boats, like real ships, know no sense of time. They know the waters, and these waters are calm.

I jump down from the rock ledge and land in the sand, fingers still entwined with Grayson's. He doesn't let go and neither do I. It's such a bold move, the connection between our hands and our palms and the way he flicks his gaze to my eyes to wordlessly make certain I'm feeling the same thing that he is. That electricity, that prickle of pleasure, crawls up my neck; everything revolves around us in that split second until Jovi's bark breaks through the quiet lapping of the water and the beating of my own heart.

Grayson's wide smile melts me into a theoretical puddle of seawater.

"Is this okay?" He whispers the words, barely audible over the waves, glancing down at our hands, then back up.

I nod, any words I was thinking of saying caught in my throat. It's more than okay. It's making me feel things in the pit of my stomach and behind my ribs that I never thought I'd feel again. That I didn't think I'd have permission to feel. And even though I can feel Caitlyn frowning all the way from another province, I have to admit for at least a second that it feels good. Not the part where she's going to be mad, but feeling the touch of a man's skin on mine, on purpose.

We walk along the length of the beach in silence for a few minutes, the dogs chasing around and behind us by the water's edge. As they gallop across the beach and ahead of us toward the dockyard, they spray Grayson and me with salty brine and particles of damp sand. Even still, we don't talk until Jovi and Perdita are past us, little dog-shaped dots in the otherwise empty distance. Our hands, though, they paint a quiet picture with gentle squeezes and delicate thumb movements.

"Maggie?" Grayson finally murmurs through the sounds of the seashore, stepping over a stray piece of driftwood as he says my name.

"Yeah?"

There's hesitation in his voice, and for a second, I think he's going to let my hand go and tell me that there's been a mistake. But he doesn't let go; instead, he pauses the circle his thumb has been tracing. "Are you really going to paint one of my photographs?"

Relief twitches at the corners of my lips. "I want to, if that's still okay."

"It's okay. I just wasn't sure if you were being nice or if you actually liked them. I've only shown my photos to a few people before. It's more of a quiet hobby than anything serious, but knowing you want to paint one of them really means something."

I look over into Grayson's blue eyes that are still sparkling in the morning sunlight. I'm about to respond when my phone begins ringing from my pocket. I know it's not Josie since we were just texting, so the only other option is a wrong number... or Caitlyn. I have no desire to answer either one of those calls at the moment, but Grayson's gaze softens and he drops his hand slowly, breaking the spell I'm under.

"I should see who that is. Just in case. It's probably Caitlyn." I pull the device from my pocket and, sure enough, her name is blinking on the screen. I punch the call answer button with a pang of regret at losing Grayson's gentle touch. "Hello, Caitlyn."

"You never called me back." Her voice is flat.

"I didn't know I was supposed to. I thought later meant I could call you back at a more convenient time."

"Well, what's so inconvenient about now?"

I'm not quite certain how to answer that question. If I tell the truth, then she's going to know I'm with Grayson. If I lie and say I'm alone, she's going to start asking questions. It comes down to if I want to answer questions now, or if I want to respond to them later.

Unfortunately, Caitlyn answers for me. "You're with him, aren't you? The other man?"

"He's not 'the other man,' Caitlyn. He's..." I pause and look over at Grayson, who is doing his best to pretend to not be listening, looking out into the distance at Jovi and Perdi who are running back toward us. "He's not."

"What do you think Taylor would say about this? Why aren't you worried about what other people will think of you turning into some easy woman, going out with the first man who comes along after your husband's passed on? Why aren't you worried what I..." Caitlyn sounds as if she's on the verge of crying, her voice cracking in the middle of her sentence. "Did you not love him as much as you said you did? Taylor loved you so much, you know that?"

Tears sting the corners of my eyes and I turn away from Grayson and the dogs to face the middle of the ocean. Lowering my voice, I respond. "I loved him, Caitlyn. I loved him with my whole heart. But his letter—his letter told me to move on. That it's okay to move on. That he wants me to be happy."

"Why can't you be happy and alone? What about your wedding vows? What about forever?"

I choke on my own tears, coughing to clear my throat as I think about the ring on my finger. "I can love him forever and still move forward. That's what the resource therapist was for. To give me the tools to help me live my life again."

Caitlyn's voice gets louder and louder. "I don't think what the *resource therapist* meant was for you to forget Taylor existed."

I can't hold my frustration back any longer, though I keep my tone as even as possible despite my broken sobs. "And you know what, Caitlyn? I don't think what Taylor would have wanted would be for us to constantly argue about his existence and the way I feel about him. I miss him every day. Every single day. But you know what? Maybe I've met someone who I have feelings for. Maybe that man has feelings for me. I don't know where it's going but all I know is that my ship is in calmer waters right now and I just want to let myself sail."

"That makes absolutely no sense."

With that, there's a click indicating the call ending, and two beeps echo in my ear to tell me that she's hung up.

I shove the phone back in my pocket, heaving out a sigh, and stare at the twinkling gray-blue of the ocean for a moment. Grayson appears by my side, manifesting from the few feet away he probably was throughout the course of the conversation. I almost forgot that he was even there, and now there's heat in my face as what I've said comes to the forefront of my mind. Luckily, he doesn't mention it right away, leaving the embarrassment to settle in my stomach. Did I really just announce out loud on the mostly empty beach that I have feelings for him?

"Everything okay?" Grayson's voice is low and he stands close, so close our hands are almost touching again.

Stifling another sniffle, I reply, "Just Caitlyn being Caitlyn. It's hard to explain."

"It sounds like she's having some difficulty managing her own feelings and she's taking it out on you."

"I don't know. I mean, maybe I'm wrong." I switch from looking at the water to the side of his face, tracing the line of his jaw with my gaze. "Maybe it's too soon. And I'm sorry she thinks of you the way she does."

Grayson takes a small step away from me to put more of a gap between us. The action sends a small pang through my chest—I don't want him farther away. I want him closer. He clears his throat. "I'm more concerned with what you think of me than the way she does. You don't get to pick your family, but it's important to take their thoughts and opinions into account."

Jovi and Perdi run behind us, kicking up more sand clumps that hit me in the back of my legs. The two of them are oblivious to everything going on, though I wouldn't expect dogs to understand the human concept of something not being a long enough time. However, I'm not oblivious to what's happening and neither is Grayson, and it makes me wonder if Caitlyn is just an obstruction to my happiness. Perhaps Caitlyn's the kind of person who wants to be sad forever, but I'm not. I can't be. And unlike what she said about being happy and alone, well, that's another story entirely.

"Maybe I should just cut things off with Caitlyn. Maybe it doesn't make sense for us to keep talking anymore." I wind Jovi's leash absently around my hand, again and again,. The lead is too tight, turning my hand red and squishing the band around my finger, but it's a distraction from the threatening tears in my eyes. "But she's all I really have left of Taylor, you know? Plus, she's the only family I have left at all. It feels like I shouldn't let that go, even if it makes me miserable sometimes."

"Then don't. I think you should consider what she's saying. But considering it doesn't mean that you have to accept it as your truth. And maybe that's something you should tell her."

"Maybe."

We gaze out into the horizon for a few seconds, neither of us saying anything, the sound of the lapping waves the only noise. I shift my weight from one foot to the other as I loosen Jovi's leash around my hand, feeling the blood flow return from my arm down to my fingers. I'm not entirely sure what to say, because there's a metaphorical boulder between Grayson and me, one that's squashing my heart and making me want to spurt out that I'm developing feelings for him that I don't know what to do about.

He sucks in a deeper breath, and I imagine the sea salt air going deep into his lungs. "Maggie?"

"Yeah?" I think I know what's coming, just judging by the way he's absently rubbing his hand along his stubbled jaw.

"I've been having feelings for you too."

The world melts into a palette of blues— Grayson's eyes, the sea, the sky. I find myself swimming in the former as I look toward him, slowly accepting the words as he's spoken them. He's been having feelings too. For *me*.

"What kind of feelings?" The question falls from my mouth before I have a chance to stop it, and it sounds just as stupid when I repeat it in my head as I'm certain it sounds out loud.

He stifles a chuckle, and he offers me a smile. "You know the kinds of feelings, I think."

"I mean, there are so many feelings."

"Well," Grayson starts as Perdi runs a circle around us and stops at his side. "Why don't you tell me about the way you feel first, and then we'll see if we're on the same page. We can walk and talk?"

Moving somewhere instead of standing still sounds like the perfect idea, and we step away from the water's edge and back up the beach a little way until we're heading back toward the dockyard with two panting dogs in tow. Sand squishes underneath my shoes as Grayson bumps into my shoulder, the movement soft and calculated, because as our arms touch, our hands brush. A tingling circulates around my body like when I have too much wine, and I cautiously run my finger along Grayson's thumb in such a way that it could feel like an accident.

It's not an accident, and he knows it.

Grayson slips his hand into mine, and we walk for another thirty seconds before he prompts me. "So, tell me about these feelings."

"I don't know what there is to say. They're good feelings. Strange in a way, but good."

"Strange how?"

I bite the inside of my lip, chewing a little before I respond. "It's just different having feelings about someone who isn't Taylor. It feels like I'm doing something wrong. It feels like I'm supposed to just paint and be alone forever, and I don't want that."

The corner of his lip quirks up in a smile as I sneak a glance. "What do you want then?"

I manage to shrug without forcing Grayson to let go of my hand. "I don't know, what does everyone want? To be happy? I want that, too. And honestly, every time I'm with you, you make me happy. Whether it's meeting on purpose or not."

He laughs then, the sound echoing over the beach. "We do seem to meet accidentally on a somewhat regular basis."

"I'm starting to think that it's not an accident."

"Maybe in the beginning it was. I don't think it is anymore, though."

I trace my gaze along his form, trying to avoid thoughts I'm not sure I'm prepared to have yet. There's something about the shape of his arms, and the movement of his mouth that makes me feel a certain way in my stomach. It's been a long time since I've kissed someone other than Taylor—years and years—but there's also something about the way Grayson bites at his bottom lip while he's thinking that makes me feel *things*.

Jovi startles me back to reality by plunking his cold nose against the back of my free hand, taking up his walk at my heel. Even though I'm dropped back outside of my short daydream, that sensation in my stomach persists and stems from the connection I have with Grayson between my other fingers.

"What do you think it is now?" I ask, stopping again along the shoreline.

Grayson looks down at me, Perdi following his position and taking a seat by his legs. Jovi wanders, and my glance follows him for a second until Grayson uses his free hand to reach up and brush my chin, tipping my face toward him. The movement is so gentle but so compassionate that I feel myself melting into a puddle in his palm the second he touches me. It's so wrong feeling this way, isn't it? But something about it is so right.

Taylor wants me to be happy.

Grayson makes me happy, and if we kissed right now, well, I don't know how I'd feel. But my body is telling me that I want it. It's been telling me that I want him to kiss me for days, and I haven't been listening. I'm listening now. I hear it. But I'm frozen to the spot and I can't move because he's touching me with both hands and my pulse is banging in my ears.

"I think…" He pauses, delicately gazing into my eyes with the summer sun reflecting off his skin. "I think that it's serendipitous. I think that maybe Taylor knew something about us before he sent that letter. Maybe he thought… I don't know. You know better than I do how hard it was to get into Taylor's head. It's impossible to say what he was thinking. Maybe it was nothing. Maybe it was everything."

We look at each other for a long time, Grayson's hand sliding from my chin to across my cheek before tucking an errant strand of hair behind my ear. Prickles of heat gather in the spaces that he's touched, like goosebumps, only they are made of fire. And as we get lost in each other's eyes, I think about leaning forward and pressing my lips against his right here on this beach.

Grayson must be able to read my mind, because after a second, he drops his hand from my neck and lets out a small cough. "Maybe we should head back? It's getting late and I should probably, I mean, you probably have things to do."

My stomach sinks, but I do my best to hide my disappointment at this not being the right time. "Yeah. I think the dogs are tuckered out. Might as well turn around."

Our fingers still linked, we alter our course in the sand and make our way back to the dunes.

Chapter Twelve

After another quiet goodbye, this one held at the driver's side door of Grayson's black hatchback, Jovi and I head back up the grassy hill to our house. Every step with my right foot I have Caitlyn's words and Grayson's advice on my mind. Every step with my left makes me wish I was brave enough to kiss Grayson to see what it would feel like. Maybe it would feel like nothing at all. Maybe it would feel like the crashing waves of the ocean, trying to tip over my grief boat into a sea of murky blue. Maybe I'd never want to do it again.

I'm taking off my sand-filled sneakers in the house before I realize I've been stuck in my own head since leaving Grayson and Perdita. Jovi's already plunked himself on the couch with a squeaky stuffed duck, honking away on the toy as I pull my phone from my pocket. The device has no notifications, but my brain recalls two things: one, that I need to text Josie back, and two, that I really should call Caitlyn and have a conversation about how we can make our lives easier going forward.

I decide to tackle the much easier conversation with Josie before I even think about calling Caitlyn back. Pulling a bar stool out from the kitchen island, I peer down into my morning's teacup in a moment's contemplation before I punch in my passcode and send a message over.

Maggie: I'm home.

Josie: Details! I totally need to know what happened. I've been holding my breath over here.

Maggie: We went to that exhibit on the waterfront. Nocturne. Nothing happened.

Josie: What do you mean nothing happened? That sounds like something happened.

Staring down at the message bubbles on the screen, I tilt my head to the side like Jovi does when I hold a treat and don't give it to him fast enough. What does she mean, that it sounds like something happened? It's not like Grayson and I kissed, even though we got awfully close to it this morning. But this morning isn't last night, and so that probably doesn't even count. Even if it does, I'm not sure I want to tell Josie about it yet. I kind of want to hold it close to my chest and revel in the feeling it gave me when I thought about Grayson's lips pressing against mine.

Maggie: Not really. Nothing serious.

Josie: I think you're underestimating the whole situation.

Josie: He's into you, Maggie.

She's not wrong, but I only know that because I raised my voice at Caitlyn and she raised her voice at me, and Grayson heard the conversation—namely the part where I mentioned having feelings for him.

I have to take a sip of my tepid tea before I can think of anything to say back to Josie.

Maggie: Maybe you're right.

Josie: Of course I'm right about this. But I guess the bigger question is, how do you feel about it?

Maggie: It's confusing.

I want to say more, tell her that it's breaking my heart and putting it back together all at once. But I don't know why there's something stopping me, as if that feeling is private, too. Like the almost-kiss is something that's just my own, the status of my heart seems personal.

Josie: He wouldn't be mad at you, you know.

Her words echo the sentiments from the second page of the letter, Taylor's words I only just read last night. However, they're the opposite of Caitlyn's statements, the ones that have hurt me most recently.

Maggie: I think I'm accepting the idea that he wouldn't be. Now it's just accepting I don't have to be mad at myself.

Josie: You'll get there. And Grayson seems patient enough to wait and understand, based on what you've told me.

Maggie: I hope you're right.

Josie: Listen, I've got to get ready for work. Try not to stress. This isn't about forgetting Taylor. It's about remembering that you're still here.

Josie and I text a quick goodbye before I set my phone facedown on the counter and absently take another sip of cold herbal tea. I can't help but think over her words and Grayson's from this morning, counter-balancing them with Caitlyn's outburst. I don't know how long I sit there, but it's at least until Jovi squeaks his toy from the couch and it startles me, nearly causing me to choke on my final mouthful of tea.

"What should we do today?" I ask him, knowing full well that I'm not going to get a response. It doesn't matter though—talking to the dog has provided me comfort in the quiet of the house ever since Taylor passed.

Jovi bites down on his toy again, the stuffed animal making a sound resembling a tea kettle. He's clearly going to be occupied for the next little while, resting there on the couch cushions with paws covered in sand, at least until I provide him with something more interesting to do.

Rising from my seat at the island, I pick up my cup and move it into the empty sink. Taylor used to joke that my version of cleaning often consisted of just moving things from one place to another, and the fleeting memory makes me smile.

My phone pings with a new email, and I cross the kitchen to flick open the app and see who it's from. I have a couple of unanswered messages from overnight, but I flick past the junk mail toward the new commission request from my online platform. There's an attachment to the email from a woman named Darlene Cross, looking for a painting of a bridge over a small river. As most of my commission emails do, this one tells me a story behind the photograph—it's an old Polaroid snapshot of Darlene's childhood play place in the woods of Nebraska. The photograph is fuzzy with time and probably also from a sub-par scanner or old cell phone, but I think I can work with it. It's nothing in comparison to the clear, sharp pictures that Grayson sent to me last night, but it's definitely not the worst I've been sent.

Darlene Cross says that she's in no rush for the painting to be completed, and she's provided me with her contact information and mailing address. Everything that I could need is in the email, and since she's said she's in no big hurry, I close the email and flag it for follow-up later on in the week. Today I want to work on Grayson's photograph of the stormy-looking ocean, the deep blues and grays and dusky whites all melting together to make the beach that I'm so intimately familiar with.

I take my phone and head down to the studio at the other end of the house, leaving Jovi and his squeaky toy behind. Pushing open the door, I am encased in the sunlight that always streams through these windows at this time of day in the summer. It streaks along the floor and up the farthest wall, and the warmth of the space is like being embraced in a familiar hug.

It takes me a few minutes to select the photo of Grayson's that resonates with me the most, and I print off a copy on my printer for reference before pulling a pre-stretched canvas from underneath one of the workshop tables. Once I begin to mix paints and try to match the hues to those in the photograph, I get lost in the moment and hours go by. The only reason I pause is to let the colors dry, and because my stomach is rumbling something fierce. When I pick up my phone from one of the aged accent tables to check the time, it's about six in the evening and I've missed lunch, and am approaching missing supper as well.

Standing back and looking at my work so far, I'm pleased with the mixture of the colors and the reflection of the sky in the water. The beach texture looks as if I could reach out and touch it, and the grayish-blue is cool and reminds me of impending thunder and lightning. I hold up my phone and snap a photo of the progress, and then quickly—before I can change my mind—send the picture to Grayson.

Maggie: Thought you might want to see what I've been working on today. (1 attachment)

I scroll through our past conversation, reading the words over and over again, hoping that I'm not interrupting something that he's doing that might be important. There's an anxious feeling in my stomach from having texted him first, like it's something I'm not supposed to do, even though the concept of him being the man and having to take the lead is so old-fashioned I don't know why I'm thinking it. Thankfully, after a few flicks of my finger on the screen, Grayson's reply pops up.

Grayson: Wow, Maggie. That looks amazing. I can't believe how real the colors are. I bet it looks even more wonderful in person.

Maggie: I'm pretty proud of this one, if I'm being honest. I got a commission today but I really felt inspired by these photos and wanted to do something for me instead of for someone else.

Maggie: Is that selfish? I feel like that might be selfish.

Grayson: Not at all. You can't do everything everyone else wants all the time. You have to live sometimes for yourself as well. And I really think that painting would look nice on that new blue wall of yours in the living room.

The message makes me smile. I hadn't thought about putting the painting somewhere in my own house, but he's right, with the colors and the shades of the ocean, it would fit perfectly along the wall in place of the emptiness that's there at the moment.

My stomach rumbles again in the quiet as I write back, my nails clickety-clacking on the tempered glass. I've just hit send back on my short message when another text from Grayson pops up.

Maggie: I think you're right.

Grayson: Did you eat supper already?

I shift my weight from one tired foot to the other, the lowering sunlight at my back. Is this another invitation for food? Or is this casual conversation?

Maggie: I didn't. Did you?

Grayson: Not yet. I was thinking of barbecuing some burgers and corn. I make seriously mean grilled corn.

Grilled corn sounds amazing, and I roll the thought of running to the supermarket over in my mind for a moment until I receive his next message.

Grayson: Would you want to come over?

Nothing that I start to type back seems to have the right tone. Not "yes," not "I'd love that"... not anything. I don't want to sound too eager after my mishap yelling about my feelings for him on the beach, and the moment I begin to think about that, I recall my entire conversation with Caitlyn and hate myself all over again.

I'm certain my typing bubbles have popped up on his screen and disappeared at least five times.

Grayson: I understand if you're not comfortable.

Maggie: It's not that. Sorry. I'm just thinking. Trying to figure out the right response, honestly.

He replies with a smiling emoji, complete with blushing cheeks.

Grayson: Call me?

Maggie: Okay.

Poking the phone icon next to his name at the top of the screen, I wait a moment for the sound of ringing. Barely half a tone gets out before Grayson's deep voice answers.

"Hey." The timbre of his voice sends a little shiver up the back of my neck, and the baby hairs stand on end like they do when a breeze hits my skin in just the right way.

"Hi. How was your day?"

I walk across the room to the window seat, complete with my new pillows from House 'N Home. Squishing them down, I recline against the wall and look out toward the yard.

"Quiet. Since I'm off for the next couple of weeks, I've just been taking care of chores around the house. Pesky things that need doing. Installed a new tap in the kitchen today. Perdi tried to help."

"I bet she did." I chuckle, thinking about how Jovi would likely try to help with such a task, all while thinking that I'm just playing a game.

There's a pause, the sound of the two of us breathing in unison echoing over the phone line.

"I didn't mean to make you uncomfortable." Grayson breaks the quiet, his voice low. "I owe you for the chicken parmigiana and thought we could spend a bit more time together. You know, because… feelings."

A little laugh escapes me. "Feelings, huh? I suppose there are some of those floating around. And I'm not uncomfortable. I'm just… I don't know."

"Is it because of that conversation you had with Caitlyn on the beach?"

I bite the inside of my lip. "Kind of."

A moment's hesitation sits between us until he fills in the gap once again. "Did you talk to her again since this morning?"

"No. I couldn't bring myself to ruin the rest of my day. Plus, I don't know what I'd say. Maybe leaving it alone is better. At least for now. She probably wouldn't answer anyway. When she gets mad, she ignores my calls."

"Hmmm." Grayson lets out a throaty hum. "I wish I could do something for you, Maggie. But I think this is something you and Caitlyn need to sort out so you don't get into a big divide over the whole thing."

I sigh, picking a stripe of robin's egg blue paint from the corner of my thumbnail. He's right—and even though I want to ask him what he means by "the whole thing" just to hear him say the words, I don't bother. "I feel like we're already divided. Nobody will ever measure up to Taylor, and I'll never convince her that it's nothing to do with whether I did or didn't love him."

"You'll get there. She knows you loved him, I'm sure of it. I mean, I know you loved him and that he loved you and I'm significantly newer to knowing you both. But it's clear—so clear. You were everything to him, even if he was quiet about it. He was loud in that aspect of his silence."

I think about the letter on the bedside table, the one telling me things that Taylor wouldn't have ever said in person, quickly coming to the conclusion that Grayson's right again. "If she knows, why does she have to be so... *Caitlyn* about it?"

"That I can't answer for you, Maggie. She's probably trying to manage wounds of her own."

And then it clicks. Caitlyn's trying to heal not only from Taylor's death, but from losing him a second time: first, when I took him away to get married and join the Navy, and second, when he died. I've lost him once. She's lost him over and over again.

I peel another splotch of paint from my hand without thinking much about what to say next. The line goes empty with dead air as my thoughts flit about from Taylor to Caitlyn to Grayson's lips on the beach this morning, and back again.

"What're you thinking?"

I'm thinking that Caitlyn is making everything inside of me complicated. I'm thinking that I'm hungry and mixed-up and covered in paint but that I want to see you.

"Is that dinner invitation still open?" I adjust the phone from one ear to the other, the screen feeling sticky on my face.

"Of course. You want to come over?"

"Yeah. I'd like that. Just give me a bit to tidy myself up. I have as much paint on me as the canvas does, and I should feed Jovi and let him out."

"No rush. Well, maybe a little rush." I hear Grayson's smile over the phone, picturing his dimple on his cheek as he grins.

"What's the rush for? Did you already start barbecuing?" My throat slightly tightens with panic at the idea of rushing over to Grayson's looking like the mess I do at the moment. I'm not prepared for him to see me in full artist mode yet.

"Oh no, nothing like that," he replies quickly. "I just... I want to see you."

All the air in my lungs suddenly disappears, but I don't remember exhaling. There's a soft calm that overtakes my body, a smile spreading from ear to ear at Grayson's admission. "What do you want to see me so badly for?" My voice drops half an octave, a low tone that I don't recognize as my own. The part that I do recognize is that I'm flirting with Grayson, something I haven't done in a long time. And it feels *good*.

"Maggie..." Grayson lets out a muffled, clearly stifled groan. "It's not late enough at night for that voice."

"And maybe it's not late enough at night for you to be telling me that you want to see me. I can only presume there are *purposes* behind that statement."

"Purposes?" He laughs, the sound of his chuckle like a breeze over the phone, loosening me entirely. "My purpose is to feed you and maybe drink some whiskey. I'm not just nice to you for *purposes*. Tonight isn't about purposes. It never was."

"Okay, okay." I stand from my spot on the window seat, the squashed cushions immediately starting to puff up again. "I'm coming over shortly. Text me the address. Do you want me to bring anything?"

I regret asking because I don't have anything interesting to bring, and stopping at the store will only put more time in between me being alone and me seeing Grayson.

"Will do. And just yourself, please."

Heading toward the hall, I step through the threshold before shutting the studio door. "I can do that. See you in a bit."

"Bye, Maggie."

I know there's a stupid grin on my face as I click the "end call" button because my cheeks are sore. But I can't wipe the smile away even after going to the kitchen to feed Jovi, or following a lengthy session at the sink trying to wash the various shades of paint from my fingers and palms. I use my orange-scented scrubby soap halfway up my arms until my skin is red and clean and smelling like citrus before I retire to the bathroom to put on a little makeup and turn the curling iron on to take out the ponytail bump in my hair. A half hour later, I'm heading out the door toward 39 Lark Avenue on the other side of Eastern Port.

"Be a good boy," I say to Jovi as I give him a pat on the head before sliding through the entryway and locking up. It's pushing seven p.m., the evening light of summer casting fading yellow patterns on the side of the house and car. Despite the fact that the sun is lowering along the horizon, it is still hot and I'm glad I've decided to wear a tank top—but I also bring a sweater, just in case.

My stomach does cartwheels all the way to Grayson's house at 39 Lark Avenue, a tiny back street filled with new construction and fenced-in yards and manicured gardens. It's much fancier than my little old house by the beach, but less personal in some ways. I park my car in the gravel driveway before turning off the key in the ignition, sitting for a moment in the driver's seat with the window down and the scent of barbecue flowing along on the breeze. I can't tell if it's coming from Grayson's backyard or somewhere else, but it sure smells good.

My belly rumbles again, and I unbuckle my seatbelt before heading to the front of the home. The storm door is open but the screen door is shut, sounds of clanging around in the kitchen drifting down the steps of the split entry and making their way outside. I knock on the edge of the doorframe, and Grayson's voice calls out from the shadowy interior as Perdita bounds down the steps to stick her nose at the mesh.

"Come in, Maggie!"

I open the door and step into the coolness of the house as Grayson wipes his hands on a dish towel, sleeves rolled up to his elbows. "Hey," I start, scratching Perdi behind the ears as I attempt to simultaneously take off my sandals. "Sorry to make you wait."

"Not a problem. Burgers and corn are on. Want a shot of whiskey while we wait?"

"You're getting right down to business, I see." Laughter twitches at the corners of my lips as I ascend the stairs and enter the open concept kitchen area with Perdi on my heels. Grayson shrugs, picking up a bottle of amber liquid. "But yes, I'll have one."

I vow to myself to keep the alcohol at a limit so I can drive home later, but a shot of whiskey with supper can't hurt, right?

He measures out two drinks and slides one along the kitchen counter toward me, a spilled droplet slipping along the side. "Cheers, Maggie."

"Cheers."

We clink our shot glasses together and gulp down the whiskey in one fell swoop, as if everything about tonight depends on it.

Chapter Thirteen

We sit outside in matching Adirondack chairs as the barbecue slowly cooks our dinner, the heat on low and the scent of grilling sauce and butter floating into my nostrils. Grayson's hand sits only inches away from mine on the armrest, fingers clasped around another cup of whiskey. He's made us something called Apple Cider Whiskey Punch, which is a mixture of the two namesake ingredients along with lemon juice and ginger ale. At the bottom is a ball of ice that he's made in a special tray, and it rolls around, tinkling against the glass as I swirl my drink and take a sip.

Grayson and I don't say much of anything important for a little while, nursing the alcohol and staring out over the back porch railing toward the trees and a little blue patch of ocean. Every once in a while, he gets up to poke at the food on the barbecue, adjust the heat, and then carefully drag out a mouthful of the punch and swallow. I remind myself that I shouldn't drink too much even though I'm enjoying the taste, the voice in the back of my head saying that it's not proper to get drunk before dinner has even been served. That rule doesn't apply to him, since we're at his house and he doesn't have to drive back across town.

Soon, the plates clatter on the patio's side table and he puts a burger and a tinfoil-wrapped cob of corn on each one before passing one over to me.

"Anything you want on your burger?" He flicks the knobs on the front of the barbecue and then spins the dial on the propane tank to turn everything off.

"I'm good, thanks."

"Just plain?" Grayson furrows his brow in contemplation, like he's trying to decide if I'm saying that I like my burgers with nothing on them so I don't inconvenience him into getting me anything from the fridge.

I nod, placing the top of the bun over the perfectly cooked burger with a smile. "Just plain. I don't like food with too many ingredients. Complicates things for my mouth."

Mirroring me, Grayson plunks the top of his bun on his burger as well and takes a seat in his Adirondack chair.

"I didn't mean you had to eat yours plain too." I delicately unfurl the edges of the tinfoil to expose the buttery, peppered corn to the summer breeze. Everything smells delicious and it reminds me of a saying of Taylor's when we started cooking together: food always tastes better when it's free and you don't have to cook it yourself.

"I like mine plain as well. I'm not much for condiments. I prefer the taste of the spices in the meat." He offers me a wide smile before he carefully unwraps his corn, doubling the buttery aroma around us.

The corn is still too hot to eat, so I take a small bite into the burger just in case it's too warm. The temperature is perfect, and the burger is juicy and spiced to perfection: a little garlic, some onion, a bit of Cajun spice. I was never great at making meat taste good without topping it with cheese, but Grayson's got some talent in the kitchen that makes me feel as if my chicken parmigiana wasn't the best thing I could have served him.

Maybe I should have filled him up with more wine first. I mentally slap myself in the head at my mistake, but then again, how could I have known that he was a proper cook?

"What do you think?" he finally asks, just as my mouth is full with my third or fourth bite of hamburger. I bob my head as I try to both savor the meal and swallow as fast as possible so I can respond.

"Really good, Grayson. I see what you mean about tasting the spices. Usually, I just like things plain because I don't know how to use spices other than salt and pepper."

"Hey, there's nothing wrong with a good dose of salt and pepper."

I swap eating for another drink of the punch, watching Grayson out of the corner of my eye as he toys with the corn and takes a crunchy bite. I would've thought that there would be no possible way for someone to look attractive while eating corn on the cob, but he manages to find a way to the point where I'm hesitant to eat my own, certain I'll look like a horse trying to nibble oats. I finish my burger before rolling the corn around in the tinfoil and coating it in more melted yellow liquid.

Of course, when I taste the corn, it's every bit as good as the burger.

"Listen, Maggie." Grayson places his crumb-spattered plate on the deck by his feet. He takes a drink from his nearly empty glass, licking at his bottom lip before speaking again. "I wanted to talk to you about something."

My heart skips at least three beats. I do my best not to react to the banging in my chest as I position my gnawed corncob atop the wrinkled tinfoil before lowering the plate onto the boards next to my own chair. "What about?"

The sun is lowering past the trees in the backyard, the blue of the sky replaced by the familiar egg yolk yellow that reminds me of Taylor, and the mug that I dropped last week. The pang behind my ribcage returns, and I have a feeling that this isn't good news, even if I desperately want it to be. It's probably about my outburst at the beach with Caitlyn. It has to be about my outburst at the beach with Caitlyn. There's nothing else. There can't possibly be anything else.

"I wanted to talk to you about Taylor. About something that happened the day that... the day he was lost at sea."

I don't know what to say because I'm shocked into silence. What would Grayson possibly want to say to me about the day Taylor died? Is there something that he knows? What's there even to know, anyway?

"Would that be okay? I've had something on my mind since the exhibit and I wasn't sure how to bring it up."

I swallow hard, trying to wet my suddenly parched throat. "You... you want to talk about Taylor's death?"

Grayson nods. "If you're ready to hear it."

Hesitation seeps through my veins and ricochets around my insides. I don't know how to take those words coming from him, maybe because I'm not certain what they're supposed to mean. If I'll *let* him talk about Taylor? What's left to talk about but the circles I've led him around and around in over the past few days? What's left to talk about except emotions and Caitlyn's anger and my inability to understand and cope with the way I've been given Taylor's permission to feel?

"I mean, I guess? It depends."

His finger slips over the condensation on the glass. "I don't want to hurt you. I never want to hurt you. After seeing you break at receiving that letter from Taylor, I don't want to make anyone feel that way ever again."

"That wasn't your fault, Grayson. That wasn't anyone's fault."

"I know. But maybe this is."

I furrow my brow and gulp down the remainder of my punch, throat burning as I set the cup down on top of the plate. When I straighten in my chair, Grayson's looking at me with pain in his eyes. It's similar to the day he delivered the handwritten note from beyond the grave, but now I see flecks of gray sadness in the clear blue. I can't help but wonder what he sees when he looks at me, hair tousled in the summer air, my curls probably fallen out, and peppercorns between my teeth. Something tells me that it doesn't matter, though.

"Just tell me what it is that you're talking about." The words come out of my mouth slowly and quiet, almost a whisper, like I know bad news is coming but I can't put my finger on what to expect.

Grayson nods toward my empty glass. "You want another of those first?"

I look down, fetch the cup, and look back up again before holding it out. The ice ball rattles against the side. Grayson's fingers brush mine as he takes the glass from me, but instead of feeling an electric warmth rush over my hand, there's a coolness to his skin that wasn't there the last time we touched. His face is blank as he turns back to the house, walking through the patio doors and gently pushing Perdi out of the way so she doesn't come out onto the patio.

He doesn't stay inside for long, just long enough to give me an opportunity to panic about what it is that he's going to say. I'm barely able to pull together coherent thoughts, fingers drumming on the arm of the Adirondack chair in a quick rhythm until he returns with two glasses that are more than half full of whiskey mixture. He hands one to me and I immediately take a gulp, that burning feeling coiling down my throat as the flavors of apple cider and ginger ale compete.

Chewing on his bottom lip, Grayson takes a seat again, rolling the melting ice ball around in his glass. "It's complicated, Maggie."

"I've come to realize everything is. Relationships, emotions, grief ships..."

"Grief ships?" He draws his eyebrows together as he pokes at the ice with his pointer finger.

"Never mind. It's not important." I swallow another too-large mouthful of punch, and this time I feel the alcohol flowing underneath my skin and through to my fingers and toes. "What were you going to say?"

Grayson sighs before he sets down his whiskey and stands again. It's almost as if he can't stay still, the words he wants to say rattling around inside of him and threatening to come out on their own if he doesn't release them. "Let me show you something."

Before I have any time to react, he lifts the hem of his shirt, exposing the tan of his stomach along with the lines of his abdominal muscles. His fingers graze the fabric, pulling higher and higher, revealing nearly his whole bare chest, a breath hitching in my throat. However, once I look—I mean, really look—I see what he's trying to show me. A scar slices his side, a puncture at one end, and a thinner mark of white trails down several inches before disappearing.

I almost reach out to touch it, to feel the texture of the skin and release the pain it must have caused him however long ago it happened. But I don't. I don't because I'm confused. What does this have to do with Taylor?

Locking eyes with Grayson, he slowly lets down his shirt again, waiting for something to sink in that just isn't coming to me. Maybe the shot and the second glass of Apple Cider Whiskey Punch are affecting my ability to understand what he's getting at, or maybe his lack of explanation isn't doing me any favors.

Slowly, Grayson's words are let out into the world. "I got that the day of the shipwreck."

Silence. A loud sort of silence that echoes in my ears, blood pumping hard as I watch him sit down and take an absent drink from his glass. There's nothing for me to say because I still don't understand, and everything for him to say because he does.

"Maggie." He says my name but he isn't looking at me. "I was there during that shipwreck. I was on the boat too."

I don't take in the words at first because I'm too busy feeling them. Feeling the letters all over my body, beating on my skin like the hard water from a shower on a sunburn. Sensing the implication of what Grayson's telling me, the scar on his stomach burned into my retinas in an attempt to show the most vulnerable part of himself. It doesn't make sense at first, Grayson being with Taylor during the shipwreck, because Grayson's still here, and Taylor's very much not.

"What are you saying?" I don't recognize the voice that comes out of me, the tone warbly and laced with tears.

Grayson reaches over and gingerly touches my hand on the armrest, his fingers lightly grazing the back of mine. I nearly pull away, something in my head much less concerned with the touch I've been craving and more concerned with the words he's just said, along with the others he's yet to say.

"I tried to save him. But there was smoke, and there was a shard of sheet metal in my side. I was bleeding, everyone was bleeding..." He trails off for a moment, choking up only for a second before quickly composing himself. His finger lifts from my hand, and I immediately wish that it hadn't because emotions are hitting me hard and fast. "I tried, Maggie. I really tried. But he was gone."

I'm numb in the most uncomfortable way, my brain trying to process the invisible words floating through the air. "How do you know? What if he wasn't?"

Grayson looks at me with a stony gaze, the kind of glance a boulder would have if it could express sadness. "Maggie. He was *gone*."

A tear slips from my eye, dangling on my lower eyelashes for a moment before dropping down my cheek. Then one more comes, and then another. Soon there is a flood of tears streaming down my face in burning rivers, and my chest heaves with sobs of realization. I wasn't there in Taylor's final moments, but Grayson was. Grayson tried to save him. Grayson felt the crash and heard the shipwreck in his ears and felt the shaking in his body that I can only imagine shook the entire frigate. And, somewhere in the back of my mind, I know now that Grayson probably also would hate the fine print that used to be visible on my paint tube which called a particular shade "lemon balm." That's because the word "balm" is too close to "bomb," and the thought of anything being entirely wrecked is too close to his memories of last summer.

Our memories of last summer.

They aren't mine alone anymore, they're shared. Two different perspectives of the same event, and the very real experience that somehow, even though I've been trying to push it away, I'm falling for Grayson and he's falling for me despite only having been brought together by Taylor's death.

Out of the corner of my eye, I see Grayson wiping at his face with the back of his hand. He sniffs once, clearly trying to hold his emotions in, but it all barely registers with me as I cry. Suddenly I don't care about my messy hair in the breeze or that I probably have pepper in my teeth. All that matters at this moment is that I've learned that Taylor wasn't alone when he died. Someone was with him. And that someone is here now.

"Grayson?" I breathe, trying to get out the two syllables without stammering in between my tears. "Were you scared?"

He nods. "I tried not to be. But in the military, there can be so much to be scared of. You push those feelings away; some of us become solid and hard and empty. I didn't want to be that way. That's why I picked up photography. It was my outlet after the shipwreck. I wanted to see beautiful things again."

I swipe my finger underneath my eyelashes, catching droplets on the skin that I wipe off on my shorts. There's a little wet smudge that's left behind. "I think that's why I painted the wall in my house. I didn't want to remember the color anymore. Painting became a way to cope. To Taylor, it was just a hobby I could take with me that made us a little extra on the side. Now, I paint because I have to. I don't know anything else. And maybe, in some ways, I'm scared too."

"Scared of what?" Grayson twists in his seat, placing his arm over the edge of the chair as our knees brush one another's. His eyes are rimmed red with emotion.

"Of losing the house. Of not being able to move on and live again. Scared of forgetting him and the way he used to cook breakfast on the weekends and promise we'd have a dog someday. Scared of... this." I pause before gesturing in a vague way to the barely perceptible space between us. "This increasingly small gap between us. Physically. Emotionally."

"It makes me nervous too, Maggie. I never thought—when I brought that letter to your house, I didn't think this would ever happen. I hadn't planned on it happening. It just did. And I have my hesitations, I do. But my..." He stops, clamping his mouth shut.

"What?"

"I shouldn't."

I wipe another tear, the skin sore from the salt and the heat. "Please, Grayson. Please do. I need the reason for all of this to be something more than just fate testing me to see if I can get through another year without Taylor. Another year in Eastern Port, alone, with the phone calls from Caitlyn serving as my only connection to anything and anyone."

"I'm here, I'm in Eastern Port. For now. Until I go to sea again at the end of the summer."

"I know you're here, I just… the end of summer isn't that far away. And you said you had hesitations."

Grayson sighs, running a hand along his stubbled jaw. "It's too soon."

"Is it? I mean, we never know how much time we have. Tomorrow…"

"I know what could happen tomorrow."

We sit there in the glimmer of the impending night, close yet far apart. I can't help but wonder if me being here is even appropriate, if my feelings are valid, or if Caitlyn is right and I'm just looking for someone—something—to fill the void in my own emptiness. I wish I knew what was going on inside Grayson's head as well. Even though we're stuck inside ourselves, our knees brush again and we don't pull them away. That connection stays. And maybe that's the thing about our connection, it's like the invisible strings of touching knees—even when you pull them apart, there's still a tingling sensation there, a reminder of the other person that lasts even after you're separated.

"Maggie?" Grayson finally turns to look in my direction.

I continue to stare down at our knees, my bare one touching his well-worn jeans. "Hmmm?"

"I don't know what to say to make this better. To make it less... I don't know. Less of an emotional struggle. You're not the only one having a hard time with this, I just want you to know that. You're not alone here."

"Neither are you."

Our gaze finally meets, and he offers me a tight smile before lifting his drink, complete with melted ice, and swallowing half of what's left. The action reminds me that I still have a nearly full cup of my own to consume, and I run my finger along the rim of the glass. Maybe I should go home.

But if I go home now, I can't help but wonder if I'll never see him again. If we've made this whole thing too strange and too uncomfortable to want to continue pushing on. But if I stay, I'm going to drink more whiskey and have feelings that I've been trying not to have around company. I'm torn—stuck halfway between getting out of the Adirondack chair and heading back out to the car, and the other half glued to my seat with my body just barely touching Grayson's.

Then he sighs, sinking down into his seat in relaxation, sliding his opposite arm over the side of the chair with his drink in hand. The other arm reaches over toward me, palm up. I don't hesitate when I take it, and Grayson closes his fingers around mine in a connection that's less invisible than the one at our knees. This connection, the one between our skin, is a kind of unwritten, unpainted, unphotographed *something* that tells me that from now on we might have moments of loneliness, but we'll never be truly alone.

I take a drink of my whiskey punch, lifting it to my lips with my unclasped hand. It flows down my throat more smoothly than it did the first time, tasting more of apple than of alcohol. In between sips, the stars come out and punctuate the summer sky with their silvery glow. Grayson points out familiar constellations like the Big Dipper while our fingers remain entwined. I don't know how long we sit out there —long enough that he refills our drinks a couple of times—the bugs staved off unlike at my little house. We talk in low voices and tilt our heads close together, the scent of liquor on his breath.

Soon, the moon hangs heavy in the midnight blue above our heads, and I find my cup is empty again. The ice balls have all been used up and were long ago replaced with generic rectangles that don't tinkle the same way in the glass, but it doesn't matter because I think we ran out of whiskey a while back.

"I should go," I whisper under my breath, my hair tickling my shoulders amid the night air. I push it back away from my face with my free hand, tucking it to one side. The wedding ring on my finger reminds me of Taylor for a fleeting second.

"I don't think you should drive."

"I'll call a taxi. It's no problem. I don't need the car for anything urgent tomorrow anyway." There's a little slur to our voices, messy, like we're painting slightly outside the lines.

Grayson frowns in the moonlight, delicately shaking the ice in his glass. "You could stay. I have a spare bedroom. A taxi is expensive."

Looking down at the ice in my own glass, I consider the offer more than I normally would. Maybe it's the softening edge of the whiskey, or maybe it's the softening edge of me, but I nod slowly. "Okay."

He pauses then, almost as if he's re-evaluating what's just happened. He doesn't let me go, but he does lean forward to place his glass on the deck before sitting up again. "Wait."

"Grayson, it's fine." I offer him the least semi-intoxicated smile I can muster. "It must be at least two in the morning. I don't think taxis in Eastern Port even run this late. After midnight, you're out of luck."

"If you're sure, Maggie."

I look over at his eyes, sparkling and somehow still blue in the dark. "Are you?"

He gives my hand a little squeeze and stands, gently pulling me with him. The rush of the whiskey hits me then, not as hard as I expect, but it's still there coursing through my veins as I smell the aroma of vanilla and sea salt and apples and ginger on Grayson. I sink into his touch, and a half-smile twitches his cheeks as he can probably feel me finally start to relax and allow myself to need him. It seems to be enough for him, enough to make him feel as if this is okay. Enough to make me feel like I'm doing what Taylor said to do in the first two pages of his letter.

"I am."

With those two simple words, I look up at the sky, picking out the brightest, flickering star. It reminds me of a line in Taylor's letter: *And I want you to know that even if I'm somewhere up in the stars watching down on you to make sure you stay safe, it will make me and my spirit and my soul happy to know that you are happy too.*

I give that blinking star a nod as if to say "thank you" before Grayson leads me inside.

Chapter Fourteen

Our fingers still entangled, we leave the deep blue of the evening behind, replacing it with the near pitch black of indoors. The kitchen and dining room are dimly lit by the light of the moon, beams of ivory reflecting off the empty whiskey bottle on the island and making a tessellated pattern on the countertop. The clock on the stove shows the time in white numbers: two a.m. on the dot. My sense of how long had passed was right, and for whatever reason, just seeing the numbers confirming it makes me stifle a yawn.

I just hope that they come before the end of the summer, because, like Grayson hinted at tonight, time off from sea only lasts so long.

Not letting go of my hand, Grayson slowly leads me toward what I presume is the spare bedroom. The darkness of the house is accented by small lights built into the electrical plugs, guiding us toward the opposite side of the split entry. An aroma of vanilla follows, but it's faint. Maybe that's because my mouth tastes like whiskey and old apples and I can smell it, or maybe it's because I'm subconsciously too occupied with thoughts about being in Grayson's house for the night.

He flicks on a carved driftwood lamp sitting atop a bureau. Against the far wall is a light wood double bed with a blue patchwork comforter, above which are two crisp, framed photographs of the beach. Textured white curtains hang on either side of the darkened windows, while an orange and off-white striped nautical rug lies at the foot of the bed and is just barely tucked beneath a fabric bench. The patterns all go together and make the room feel beachy, open, and cozy all at the same time.

"This okay?" His voice is low and rumbling, which makes my heart do a little flip in my chest. Something about his deep tone sends me to the edge of being able to keep in control under the influence of whiskey punch, and for a moment I lose myself in the thought of kissing him right here in this bedroom under the faded glow of the lamp. "Maggie?"

I drop back down to earth, quickly responding. "Oh—yes. It's perfect."

Grayson's gaze flickers toward our hands and then back to me. "The bathroom is across here. My room is at the end of the hall if you need anything. There are facecloths and towels and extra toothbrushes in the cabinet. Light's right inside."

"You're more prepared than I expected."

"I'm in the military. It's part of my job to be prepared."

I nod, and we stand at the doorway in silence for a moment, the quiet buzz of the lamp's lightbulb humming in the background. Grayson's thumb traces lines across the back of my hand, and I do my best to hold back a yawn. The alcohol has started wearing off and I'm desperately tired, but I also don't want to lose the sensation of his fingers on my skin. And, maybe even more than that, I suddenly realize that without Jovi here, I'm going to have to sleep alone.

That shouldn't make me panic as much as it does, but I must stiffen at the thought of being alone here in a dark, strange house because Grayson frowns and takes a small step closer.

"Something wrong?"

I shake my head, trying to relax my body, but it won't cooperate. "It's silly."

"I doubt that." He reaches for my shoulder, delicately turning me to face him. We're close, but not too close, his open palm on my bare arm. I want to step in and collapse into his warmth, but that would be too much. And no matter what, I don't want to be too much for him. "I know something's not right, but I don't know what it is and it's making me worried. Is it something else that Caitlyn said?"

"No, nothing like that. I'm... I'm working through my emotions about Caitlyn. This is... just more."

"If you're not comfortable, Maggie, I'll call up one of the guys from the ship. He'll be able to take you home. I'd drive you myself but, you know. Whiskey and all."

Biting the inside of my lip, I realize that I can't bear to look at Grayson. Swapping my gaze from his face down to the floor, I debate the awkwardness of being driven home from Grayson's house by a complete stranger versus just telling him that I'm feeling anxious about sleeping alone. I'm not sure which one is worse, but I also can't think up any alternate options. I'll make it through the night. It's only a few hours until the sun comes up. I'll be fine here by myself.

The metallic taste of blood alerts me to the fact that I've clamped my teeth hard against the skin inside of my mouth.

"Do you want me to call one of them?" Grayson's not pushy, his tone soft and compassionate. I shake my head. I don't want to be too much bother. *It's silly. I'll be fine.* He stifles a yawn before he says, "Talk to me, Maggie."

I'm too far into things now and I can't get out. My grief ship is wobbling again, exacerbated by the conversation from earlier and the remnants of alcohol in my system. I'm not going to cry, but I do recognize that my breathing has gotten erratic, and I suck in a deep mouthful of the warm house air before I finally decide that I need to speak.

"It's..." I hesitate, trying to find the words. "I haven't slept by myself since I got Jovi shortly after Taylor passed. It's just a bit strange thinking about being in a different house, alone at night."

For a moment it feels like all the oxygen has been sucked out of the room because I can't catch my breath and Grayson doesn't respond. It's only a matter of seconds, two or three at most, but then he runs his hand down my arm and takes the fingers of my other hand, my wedding band hand, in between his.

"What can I do to help? Do you want me to stay up with you?"

Some part of me wants to say yes, because the moment I'm alone I might start thinking too much about Caitlyn's comment that has definitely gotten the best of me. But when I meet his gaze, there are shadows dancing around his eyes. He can't possibly stay up all night, and it wouldn't be right of me to ask. "You're tired. You should get some sleep."

"What about you?" Grayson chews his bottom lip in apparent thought. "Would it help if I brought Perdi to sleep in here?"

The thought of having her in the room does calm my nerves a little, but the more I think about it, the more I just want Grayson here with me. "Honestly, I don't know. Maybe?" I pause again. "Actually, no. Well, this is a lot to ask…"

"What is it?" His voice is gentle, and he runs a finger along the inside of my hand. The sensation vibrates up my arm and over my chest and shoulders, sending little sparks off along my spine.

I can't ask him to stay in this room with me, and I can't ask if I can stay in his room with him, can I? But I don't want to be alone and tipsy and in the dark with my thoughts, away from the closeness and scent of the ocean to lull me to sleep.

Thankfully, Grayson puts the pieces together before I have to say a word. I'm not sure if that makes things more or less awkward, but I'm glad for it nonetheless.

"Come to my room?"

He says it as a question, but I think Grayson already knows he doesn't have to ask. I'm the one with the query, not him, and I'm the one who needs the comfort of another body in the room in order to get to sleep. It feels childlike in some ways, like sleeping with a nightlight.

"I just—I need a minute, if that's okay."

"Of course. I'll leave the door open for you. End of the hall." The corner of Grayson's lips quirks up in a subtle grin, and he gently releases my hands before turning and heading out of the room.

When he's gone, I run a hand over the side of my face and up through my hair, untangling the knots in my waves from the wind. Looking around the room for a moment, feeling absolutely ridiculous and nervous all at the same time, my heart beats a little harder in my chest.

And, of course, Caitlyn's words echo in my head.

It's only been a year, Maggie. It's only been a year.

Well, Caitlyn, it's been one hell of a year.

I step across the hallway into the bathroom, flicking on the light that's to the left of the door. The space is bright from the vanity light, casting a yellowish glow that burns my eyes as they try to adjust to the sudden change from the darkness. Closing the door, I encase myself in the small room. Remembering what Grayson said about toothbrushes, I pull down a wicker basket to find a couple of travel packages of toothbrush and toothpaste, and pluck one out before placing it next to the sink.

As I'm opening the package to brush my teeth and hopefully rid myself of the taste of old apples and whiskey, I can't help the thoughts running through my head. Flicking my gaze up to the oversized mirror, I stare at myself from the waist up. My jean shorts aren't going to be all that comfortable to sleep in, and my shirt isn't long enough to cover my underwear if I took them off. My hair is a disaster, full of knots, and the curls have long since fallen out and turned into scraggly tendrils from the flexible-hold hairspray. There's not much I can do about either of those things. I wasn't prepared to stay here, and I wasn't prepared to get so messy.

Maybe none of it will matter; perhaps there's a blow-up mattress on his floor right now waiting for me. Or maybe he really is okay with sharing his bed. It's the unknown that consumes me for longer than it should, and I realize when I pull my phone from my pocket that between having a crisis and looking at myself in the mirror, fifteen minutes have passed.

With a sigh, I clean myself up as much as I can before giving myself one last look over before turning off the light and gathering up the courage to head down the hall to Grayson's room.

The door is open and the floorboards squeak a little as I step into the wee-morning dark. Grayson's standing at the window, looking out at the backyard, the light of the moon cascading over him and onto the laminate floor and bed. I pause on the threshold, waiting for my eyes to adjust so I don't stub my foot on a piece of furniture. Directly across from me is a king-sized bed, covers pulled back, with a bureau and walk-in closet along one wall. A white rock-salt lamp glows from the side table next to some kind of plant, the color matching the glimmer of the outside light. Perdi is in her dog bed in the corner, and there's a soft snore coming from her fluffy body.

"Did you find everything you need?" Grayson turns to look at me, the moon glowing on his blond hair. He's changed into a different tight, dark T-shirt that contours to every muscle on his chest, while a pair of light gray sweatpants hang off the curve of his hips.

"Um, yeah. I did. Thanks."

Every muscle in my body is frozen as I stand there in the doorway looking at him. A voice in the back of my head is telling me that this was a horrible idea, while the voice in my heart reminds me that I can't let myself fall apart and grieve forever.

However, as my eyes adjust, I realize that there's no air mattress on the floor, no blankets and pillow on the rug next to the bed. And that's when it hits me that he's fine with me sleeping in the same bed as him. Or, at least,

I think he is. It still feels presumptuous and somewhat awkward. It's like I'm back in high school, sneaking into Taylor's room to spend the night for the first time. Except I'm not in high school now, and I haven't been in bed with a man other than Taylor since before graduation. I'm not sure what's worrying me more—the prospect of sleeping in the spare bedroom or the idea of spending the night in this room only a foot away from Grayson.

Either way, I stifle a yawn. Grayson crosses the room to one side of the bed, and I watch him crawl carefully under the covers. "Are you okay sleeping in those shorts? I can't..." His voice trails off as I look down at myself, still standing there in the doorway. It's the exact thing I was thinking in the bathroom, but something about taking my shorts off in front of Grayson seems a bit forward.

"Yeah, they're okay."

He pulls the covers away from the opposite side of the bed a little more, beckoning me. "I won't bite, Maggie. We're both exhausted and had a little too much whiskey and don't want to be alone. If you're uncomfortable, I can sleep on the rug. It's fine. No worse than the beds on the ship."

Grayson lets out a little chuckle, and the sound melts me from the spot I've been stuck in. I count my steps as I cross the room, the numbers reflecting the beats of my own heart, before I climb onto the mattress and sink into the foam pillow. It feels like I'm lying on a cloud, and I tug the blankets up around me. With the size of the bed, I can't even tell that there's someone else there with me until Grayson moves to flick off the salt rock lamp.

I curl up on my side, facing away from him and toward Perdi's bed. I'm fine for a few minutes there in the dark, but then my shorts start to cut off the circulation in my legs. They're too stiff and too tight on my thighs—not meant for sleeping in. At least if I'm thinking about the prickling pins and needles feeling along my lower half, it's a distraction from my wandering thoughts.

Adjusting my position, I try to get comfortable on my back without disturbing Grayson. That helps for a few minutes. Long enough that I can close my eyes and start to doze off, thinking about the scent of vanilla and spearmint toothpaste in the air. But it doesn't take long before the feeling comes back, the discomfort of my jean shorts, too tight on my legs and digging into my hips. Carefully, I attempt another position, moving slow so I don't jiggle the mattress.

It doesn't work.

Grayson tilts his head over his shoulder to look at me, and I can feel my cheeks burning hot with a flush of embarrassment. I don't even let him get any words out before I whisper, "Sorry, trying to get comfortable. It's these shorts. Maybe they're not as comfortable as I thought they would be. Is it okay if... if I take them off? I have proper underwear on so it's not like..."

I'm not sure where I'm going with that statement, but Grayson rolls halfway over and there's a cheeky grin on his face. "Maggie, just take them off. It doesn't mean anything. Don't overthink this."

What Grayson is saying implies that I'm not a master of overthinking things. Things like what he's thinking about me not being able to sleep by myself in that spare bedroom, and like taking off my shorts and getting into his bed with my bottom half almost naked. With a sigh, I mentally shove the thoughts to the back of my mind, as far back as I can shove them. Maybe the issue isn't that it means nothing, maybe it's that I kind of *want* it to mean something to him.

"I'm not overthinking anything. It's just... general thinking."

He rolls the rest of the way over to face me, propping himself up on one elbow and watching me for a moment like he's evaluating every thought that could be going through my head. My heart skips a beat as his shirt twists along his stomach, exposing his abdomen a little. I know there's a scar there, the one he showed me earlier, and as my gaze flicks down to peek at it, Grayson asks a question that diverts my glance to his face, and then up and away from him.

"What's going on then?"

I squish back a little harder into the soft foam and stare at the darkened light fixture on the ceiling. "It's nothing. Just sleepy, drunk, whiskey-based thoughts."

"Are you sure you don't want to talk about it?" He's still looking at me; I can sense it. Do I want to talk about it?

Do I want to let him know my very real, very conflicted feelings any more than I did on the beach? I do, but I'm uncomfortable lying here in these stupid shorts that are currently the bane of my existence.

"Can I take these shorts off first?"

He laughs quietly, probably trying to do his best not to disturb Perdi. "Of course."

Unfastening the button on my shorts, I wriggle out of them under the blankets before dropping them onto the floor. The bedsheets are cool on my skin, the fabric soft on my legs. Grayson waits patiently, pretending not to watch my clumsy movements, until I find myself tucked in and rolled over to face him from across the mattress. Turns out that having my shorts off in his bed is less strange than I thought it would be.

"Good?" His voice is deep and throaty, the word giving me goosebumps on my arms. Suddenly, without the shorts, my body wants his warmth against the coolness of the air conditioning. Not for anything intimate, but for the sake of having it, as well as the closeness of somebody I trust in my personal bubble.

"Good."

"Now, tell me what's going on in your head. I want to hear all of those thoughts."

There in the darkness, I feel as if I can finally be vulnerable with Grayson. It's as if the floodgates open and a wave washes over me, but somehow the water doesn't sink my grief boat. In fact, it makes me wonder if I'm still on a grief boat at all. "Are you sure?"

"Of course."

I hold in a yawn that he probably can't see because the moon has slightly shifted its position and is now behind a large tree, making the bedroom darker than it was before. The words don't come right away, leaving Grayson and me in a silence punctuated by Perdi's snores. That is, until I think up a very not graceful way to break the ice.

"I'm sorry I'm such a mess. I... honestly, there's never been anyone other than Taylor and I'm not sure how to get my head around all of this. All of these feelings and emotions and the way my head thinks and my body responds. Sometimes they match up. Other times they don't, and it's confusing and uncomfortable and scary. But good as well. If that makes sense."

"Letting go of some of that grief and allowing yourself to move forward is a difficult thing, Maggie. It doesn't happen overnight. It happens in waves."

The water reference makes me smile. "I know. But sometimes that wave knocks things over right away, or overnight, or faster than you'd expect."

Grayson nods, shifting his weight on the bed as he looks at me. "Are you trying to say something about what's going on between us? Are these... is this going too fast?"

"No, no." I try to take back my verbal vomit and rephrase what I was getting at. "It's more that I'm more ready than

I thought I was. I think that I was allowing myself to be swallowed up by fear and routine. Which isn't such a bad thing for a little while, but I've come to understand that I can't cover every piece of Taylor, you know? It's like painting the wall in the living room. Underneath, the paint is still yellow. Underneath, Taylor's still in my heart."

"He's not going to disappear because he's physically gone, Maggie."

I suck in a breath. "I know. I'm coming to understand that now. I'm just worried I'm starting to forget about him because... because I'm starting to think about you."

He shakes his head, reaching across the bed to touch my arm. There's a little vibration in his voice and he sniffs in a breath. "You'll never forget him."

Swiping my hair back from my face, I reach for Grayson and reply, "Neither will you."

We brush our fingers along each other's skin for a moment, feeling one another's outside coolness and internal warmth. His eyes shine in the moonlight that's managed to peek its way back around the canopy of trees, while my heart beats faster every time his hands get closer to mine. I find myself inching closer to Grayson, one little bit at a time. Then he begins to slide toward me like we're debating with our own selves as to whether or not we should close the gap that's between us in this king-sized bed. Our bodies eventually meet in the middle of the mattress, and I sink my head into the broadness of Grayson's chest, his chin resting atop my head. The familiar smell of vanilla and trees—with an edge of apple cider—wafts up my nose, and I suck it down into my lungs as deep as I can for as long as possible.

Soon, I close my eyes and synchronize my breathing with his. The rhythm of his chest moving begins to lull me to sleep, and it doesn't matter anymore that I don't have shorts on or that I was worried about being in bed with him. I wrap my arms into the gap between Grayson's chest and mine, squeezing myself into as small a package as possible. After a few more minutes pass, I tuck my legs around his, our hips aligned with one another and rocking gently with every breath.

"Grayson?"

He hums a response, telling me that he's almost asleep.

"Can I tell you something?"

Another soft mumble, a shift of weight, a pull closer into his body. I want to tell him that I'm falling for him, even though it hasn't been long. That time doesn't matter because when the right person comes around, everything drops into place. But as I lie here, curled up with him in the middle of his bed, my tangled curls tickling his face, it strikes me that he's already aware. Words aren't necessary, because our actions have already told us everything we need to know. And we know that we need one another, that we want one another, and that we're only so many touches, so many moments, and so many dog walks and dinners and glasses of Apple Cider Whiskey Punch away from completely admitting it.

Chapter Fifteen

I ALMOST EXCLUSIVELY PAINT for the next four evenings, meeting Grayson and Perdita in the morning at the beach with Jovi. Afternoons I spend with Josie, her vacation days from work coinciding perfectly with lunch dates and afternoon trips for coffee. She encourages me to tell her about the night of the barbecue over and over again while we drink single vanilla shot iced cappuccinos on the patio of A Cup or Two, pretending we're two of the tourists who have started gracing Eastern Port for the summer.

During those four days, I find myself in a new routine of complete bliss, forgetting that Caitlyn even exists—at least for the most part. I'm able to neglect any thought of her for the majority of the day, but at night when I'm in bed texting Grayson with Jovi on the other side of the bed, the memory of her comments that day on the beach begin to eat away at me.

She hasn't called me, and I haven't called her. Maybe we really are growing apart, the strides we had made in repairing our friendship replaced with frustration. It's the end of the new week when my phone rings, my hands deep in the kitchen sink washing the pots that can't go in the dishwasher. I think about ignoring the call when her name blinks on the screen, but I was always taught to be the bigger person whenever possible, and so I swipe a soapy finger across the device and hit the speaker button.

"Hello, Caitlyn."

The dishwater swishes under my hands as I continue scrubbing away at the pot with a small pad.

"Maggie. Just thought I'd call and see how you're doing."

There's a pause, the two of us obviously working hard to think of something more to say, even though she's practically handed the conversation over to me. I look up and out the window at the hazy ocean sky, considering what I should say. What I really want to do is chew her out for her attitude about Grayson last week, the attitude that's been secretly eating away at me, but that won't do anyone any good.

I decide to be pleasant and polite, but nothing more.

"I'm fine, thank you. How are things over there?"

"Oh, they're fine."

Another hesitation in the discussion, if one could even call it a discussion. Sure, we're going back and forth in some kind of conversation, but neither of us is really engaged beyond what I presume is an obligation.

"That's good." *Swish, swish, swish.* Water drips onto the edge of the countertop and I brush it away with a tea towel before it can land on the floor. An awkward silence ensues for so long that I start counting the seconds. I get to twenty-five before Caitlyn speaks again.

"Listen, Maggie. I guess I just wanted to call to apologize."

My brow furrows. "Oh?"

Another twenty seconds pass; I know because I watch the call timer count them out on the screen.

"I... I was wrong to speak to you like that last week. I just, it's hard. It's hard to see you moving on when I still feel like I'm losing Taylor more and more, day after day. Do you ever... do you ever just forget what his voice sounded like? Or the way he laughed? I feel like those things are fading away as time passes, and it... it hurts."

Setting the pot on the drying rack, I wipe my hands on the damp tea towel before picking up my phone. Caitlyn sniffles on the other end of the line, but quietly, like she's trying to hide it.

"I know what you mean." I walk across the room and take a seat on the couch, Jovi coming down the hall with his stuffed pig and plopping it on my lap. Absently, I begin to play tug of war with him, the dog unaware that he's interrupting a conversation. "I've been going through that for a while."

"So have I, but I think I responded to it with anger, whereas you seem to have a more... You have someone else now, Maggie. You've been able to move on and you got a letter from Taylor. I got nothing. I have nothing left of him other than a few Christmas cards and some memories."

"That's not nothing, Caitlyn."

"I know it's not. But sometimes it feels like it isn't enough. I don't mean to make you feel bad. And I don't mean to be jealous, but I wish that... I was important enough to be worth a note."

That Caitlyn might have been jealous of my letter never even crossed my mind. Maybe because I wasn't sure having it was a good thing. Or maybe because I was so conflicted over the fact that it brought Grayson and me together that I didn't even think that Caitlyn might be losing out on one last connection with her brother.

I breathe out a sigh. "I'm absolutely certain it had nothing to do with you not being worth the thought. I don't have a good explanation for why he only did this for me. Maybe he never had time to finish letters for anyone else."

"Somehow, I doubt that. You were always his priority, you know that. And honestly, the more I think about it, the more I'm realizing that's okay. I think—and maybe Taylor never told you about this—but after he and I had the argument after Dad passed away about him not being home, it kind of divided us. I don't want that to happen with you and me, too."

There's a pang of guilt in my chest at my previous thoughts of never talking to Caitlyn again, ones that I expressed as an option to Grayson. Grayson, who told me not to even take that into account because Caitlyn is family. But even still, I'm confused because it really did seem like for the last year that she only spoke to me out of obligation, rather than any actual desire to know how I was doing.

So, leaning back on the couch cushions after relinquishing the stuffed pig to Jovi, I ask, "Caitlyn, I've felt like since Taylor passed that you've only been calling because you'd felt like you had to."

"I understand." I hear her sniffle again, and then there's a sound like a tissue being pulled from a box. "You're not wrong. But the more I've thought about it this week, the more I've realized that being hurtful toward you isn't what Taylor would have wanted. It won't bring him back."

I nod, even though Caitlyn can't see it, and all of a sudden, my eyes get cloudy with tears. She's right. Being angry won't bring Taylor back. Ignoring one another won't bring him back either. And for a moment, I wonder if I reading the letter to Caitlyn will help her connect with him a little bit more and have something to hang on to. I know the note in Taylor's handwriting was—*is*—personal, but this breakthrough we're having hundreds of kilometers away from one another is worth the effort. After all, Caitlyn only started acting completely different after his passing, and I'm sure that I was different too.

"Do you want to hear what Taylor wrote to me?" I ask, trying to steady my breathing. "I can read it to you. I've only gotten through two of the three pages, though." I hold back sniffles as I do my best to get the words out.

Caitlyn nearly cuts off what I'm saying. "No, no, Maggie. Those words are for you. I didn't mean it like that. I just meant that sometimes I wish I had my own letter to lean on."

We stay quiet for another few moments. I have no idea what Caitlyn's thinking, but in my own head, I'm empty, just watching the rain plop off the edges of the patio railings, making puddles on the grass where the ground is uneven. For the first time in what feels like a while, my head is quiet, and a silent tear slips down my cheek. I don't bother brushing it away, instead focusing on the feeling it leaves on my skin. Almost the same as the feeling I get from the grief boat, or the color yellow, or the memories of a frigate coming into the dockyard with an invisible Taylor on board.

"I should go." Caitlyn's voice is quiet and rough, and I can tell now that she's crying. "But please tell… what's his name? Tell him I'm sorry that I was the way that… I was. I'm sure you've talked to him about this judging by, well, everything."

"Grayson," I reply, not sure what she means by the last statement but not wanting to push the point. "And I'll tell him."

"Thanks. Talk to you later."

"Bye, Caitlyn."

I tap the "end call" button and set the phone down on the couch cushion next to me, wiping my sensitive eyes with the back of my hand. After I look out at the rain for a couple of minutes, the tears dry, and a little smile breaks across my face. It's silly, smiling for a second at nothing out a drizzly window, but I know that Caitlyn's given me a blessing that I didn't even know I was waiting for. To move on with my life, like what Taylor told me to in his letter.

Thinking of the letter, I recall that there's still one more page to read. The silence of the house and the atmosphere of the rain feel like the perfect time to pick up the last sheet and see what Taylor had to say in his final correspondence.

Jovi follows me as I head to the bedroom at the other end of the house, nails clicking on the floor and reminding me that I desperately need to give them a trim. As I walk through the doorway, he hops up on the bed in his usual spot, twirling around on the blankets to make himself a nest before plopping down. I curl next to him, feet under the comforter, and reach around a murky green paint cup to collect the letter. I flip past the first two pages, setting them face-down on the bed between Jovi and me, and then take a deep breath before sinking into the words written in Taylor's blocky writing.

The words are smaller than on the other pages, like maybe he was lacking paper and time and still had too many things left to say to fit on a single page.

I'm running out of words to tell you how I feel, even though I think there are a million more things that I could say to get the same point across. But the most important thing is for you to know that you were—are—a part of me and you always will be, no matter where in the universe I am. I wish I could tell you where that is so that you'd know where to find me.

Maybe consider this: when you wish on stars from now on or see the rain or watch out the window for a ship to come into the dockyard, know I'm a little piece of you as well.

I remember once Caitlyn told us after her break-up with Marc that loving someone is like gluing together two pieces of paper and then eventually ripping them apart. The imagery always bothered me, because I never believed that we'd be apart. But now we are. And even though we have, like I said on the other pages, I just want you to be happy again. I want you to know that I'm happy too—happy that you chose to spend life with me.

All of that to say the most important thing of all, Maggie, the thing that I hope you'll keep forever as my last words: thank you for loving me.

Taylor

The title of the Bon Jovi song at the end of his letter is what sends me over the edge. Those tears that I wiped from my face after my call with Caitlyn come back, sending tiny waterfalls over my cheeks and crushing sobs in my chest. I'm certain Taylor knew what he was doing with that line, that he knew I would get the reference and it would mean everything to me as it did to him.

I set the final page of the letter down between Jovi and me, reaching over to pat his head and seek comfort in his fluffy husky fur. He seems to know that something's not quite right because he unfurls himself from his position on the opposite side of the bed and crawls onto my lap, his weight like a comforting blanket over my legs. Jovi wiggles toward my face and licks the tears from my cheek, which only serves to make me cry more because I'm certain with every passing day that Taylor would have loved this dog with all of his heart.

Unexpectedly, I don't cry for long. I though that I would have an intense emotional breakdown after reading his final words, but I don't. There are tears, of course, ones that have been waiting for the letter's conclusion. However, my grief boat is no longer the size of a cruise ship with the buoyancy of a brick. It hasn't been for some time, and maybe it took my painting and these words and dog walks on the beach and finding Grayson to finally realize it.

Swiping my hand over my face, I dry my cheeks and sigh. Jovi stares at me with his liquid eyes, head tilted to one side as if he understands.

"You would have liked Taylor, you know."

Jovi tilts his head the other way, pawing at my arm and wiggling closer to my stomach. I run my fingers over his head and behind his ears, giving him a good scratch. "Yes, you really would have liked him. He was one of those people, the strong, silent type. Firm but fair and kind. You've met Grayson and Taylor was a little like him. Grayson is a little gentler than Taylor. A little more talkative and a bit heavier on the feelings."

Talking about Grayson makes me smile, and I continue to rub Jovi's fur, soft between my fingers. "Speaking of feelings, I think you probably know I'm having some. But just because Grayson and Perdita might come around doesn't mean I'm going to care any less for you. I hope you know that."

He shifts his head down onto my thigh and lets out a little puff of air, closing his eyes.

Well, now I'm stuck here.

I fold the pages of the letter back together and gently place them in the envelope before placing it over on the side table back under the cup of paint water. I pick up my phone and look at the blank screen for a moment before I open up the message window to my previous conversation with Grayson.

Maggie: Hi.

Grayson responds right away.

Grayson: Hey, what's going on?

Maggie: Not too much. I just got off the phone with Caitlyn and then read the rest of Taylor's letter.

Grayson: Did you want to talk?

I bite my lip for a second, thinking it over. I wouldn't have messaged him if I didn't want to have a discussion about everything that's happened, but it's kind of him to ask.

Maggie: Yeah. If you're not busy.

Grayson: Never too busy for you. One minute.

Not even a full minute passes before his name blinks on the screen, and I answer on speakerphone, Jovi looking up at me but not lifting his head.

"Hi."

"Hey, Maggie. How was your afternoon with Josie? Last day of her vacation, right?" Grayson's voice is deep over the phone, and I hear Perdita bark once in the background before he hushes her.

"Yeah, last day. Back to the real world tomorrow. She's not looking forward to heading back to House 'N Home and mixing paint for the rest of the summer, but at least she's been scheduled for good shifts for the next few weeks, so she's pretty happy about that."

We don't say anything for a couple of seconds, the rain pattering on the windows and the soft beating of my heart the only sounds. I don't know how to break the conversation with Grayson because I hate that I keep bringing up my drama with Caitlyn and my feelings about Taylor. He's going to get tired of me doing that eventually, right? My worry is placated when he takes the lead.

"So, Caitlyn and the letter from Taylor. That's a lot to deal with for one day. How're you feeling about it all?"

I run a hand over my cheek. The skin is a little sore from my salty tears. "Caitlyn apologized."

"Well, that's good. About anything in particular, or just a general apology?"

"Mainly about how she felt hurt that Taylor didn't think to write her a letter too, how she's worried she's starting to forget him, and that she doesn't want to be angry anymore because that's not what Taylor would have wanted. Oh, and she said to say she's sorry to you as well."

"To me?"

"To you. For her judgment."

"Well, that's kind of her." Something in the background shuffles, and there's the creak of wood. "I'm glad that you two were able to connect in a positive way. Family can be so important, especially after a loss and during the grieving process."

"Yeah. I think I was struggling with Caitlyn's thoughts and opinions more than I let on. We've known each other since we were young and as much as it hurts to have lost Taylor, losing that connection with Caitlyn would be painful too. Even if we did feel obligated to talk to each other for a little while."

"That doesn't mean that you have to forget everything she's said, but I think a bit of forgiveness for the way she's spoken to you will go a long way."

"Me too." I shift my weight on the bed. A little smile breaks across my face as I say the final words, the sensation of freedom lifting the weight from my chest.

"I don't want you to feel rushed, Maggie. I'm not going anywhere."

A thought suddenly hits me, and that twisting, tight feeling in my chest returns. "Well, you kind of are. You said before that you're going back to sea at the end of the summer."

The quiet speaks volumes, even though it only lasts a moment.

"And I'll come back from sea in a couple of months. You'll paint more pictures of the ocean while I'm gone, I'll talk to you whenever I can, and maybe..." Grayson hesitates, clearly thinking about something that he isn't saying.

"Maybe what?"

"It's nothing in particular, just lots of maybes."

The furniture on Grayson's end of the line groans again in the stillness, and I shuffle my weight gently under Jovi's heavy body. My legs are beginning to develop a pins-and-needles sensation from my thighs down to my toes, not enough to make everything numb, but just enough that it's uncomfortable. I wiggle underneath the dog, pulling the paint-splattered blankets a little askew. I don't want to be left alone here in Eastern Port again, but I can't imagine severing the connection and the feelings I've developed for Grayson just because he's going to sea.

Suddenly, there's an emptiness in my heart that needs filling, something that only his company can provide. And it's at that moment I recognize that our time, for now, is limited and that we might as well make every moment count, not holding back, that we should be staring up into the stars, saying thank you for the days that we have because who knows when we won't get any more.

"Grayson?"

"Hmmm?"

I give myself one final push up against the headboard, disturbing Jovi just enough that he opens one eye to stare at me for daring to move. It only takes a couple of gentle pats on his head before he begins to doze off again. "Can I see you tonight?"

"Of course. But don't you have that commission you're supposed to be finishing?"

"Darlene Cross' painting? It can wait another day or so. I'm almost done. The piece I really wanted to finish was yours, and I've managed to get all the details complete and it's dry. Just need a bit of help hanging it up in the living room as *someone* suggested."

Grayson chuckles. "I'll be there soon. Want me to bring anything?"

I mentally run through the supplies I'll need. Candles, wine, a blanket, the solar lanterns from the patio. But I don't need him to bring anything. I just need him.

"Nothing. Just yourself. But meet me at the beach, okay?"

"The beach?" he asks like he's not entirely sure where I'm going with this idea.

"Yeah. The entrance by the edge of the dunes."

There's a little laugh that comes from somewhere deep in his throat, and it rings true in my ears. "I'll see you in half an hour, then. On the beach. In the dark. Definitely not ominous at all."

Chapter Sixteen

The idea that I have rolling around in my head is more intimate than I expected to feel at a moment like this one, not because Taylor wasn't romantic, but because he had a different way of showing his emotions. I grew used to how he expressed his affections and feelings, and there was nothing wrong with the way he chose to show that he loved me. It's just different than the way I want to show Grayson that I'm interested in him because saying the "L" word seems a little far off. Plus, Grayson and Taylor aren't the same people, which, in some ways, makes my attempt at being romantic a bit more anxiety-inducing than it otherwise would be.

Once we hang up, my heart is beating so fast that it makes my fingers feel twitchy. The countdown is on until Grayson arrives at the beach, and I'll have to hurry if I want to finish setting up in time.

Rushing into the bathroom, I twist my hair into a loose ponytail, swipe on some blush, and brush my teeth with the last of the orange-mint toothpaste Taylor loved while making a mental note to pick up some more when I get groceries on Tuesday. It all takes under ten minutes, leaving me with approximately twenty minutes to execute my plan. Jovi watches me from the bathroom threshold as I internally check items off the list in my head. Of course, there are a million thoughts going through my mind—namely, what if Grayson thinks I'm ridiculous? What if I've been reading him wrong all this time? I shake my head, my ponytail swatting either side of my neck as I do my best to be reasonable about this.

To be fair, Grayson did laugh and sound amused when I said for him to meet me at the beach, so if nothing else, he's at least going to humor me.

Before I head back down the hall to the kitchen, I collect some scented candles from the rim of the bathtub that smell like a combination of vanilla and citrus. Balancing them in my hands, I set them down on the kitchen island before gathering a chilled bottle of white wine from the fridge, a knitted blanket from the couch, a barbecue lighter from the junk drawer, and the small solar lanterns from the patio. They all get shoved into the largest reusable StopShop Grocery Mart bag I can find hanging from one of the hooks by the front door.

My phone beeps from the kitchen island, and I rush over to answer, knowing that I'm running low on time. Josie's name pops up on the screen and I tap the message.

Josie: I hope you have big plans with Grayson tonight. It's gorgeous out. The heat finally broke.

I immediately smile, texting her back.

Maggie: I do, actually. I have a surprise planned for him at the beach.

Josie: Sounds romantic. You're so sweet, Maggie. What's the surprise?

Reading her message over again, I realize that I don't actually have a surprise other than sitting on the beach and lighting some candles and drinking wine. But maybe I need something more than that now that I'm coming to terms with my grief and my feelings toward Grayson. At that moment, something tickles my brain, giving me the same feeling of fireworks up the back of my neck as I felt the first time that Grayson and I touched. What I really want, more than anything, is him. To feel his body against mine like on the beach that first day, but on purpose this time. To have his warm vanilla scent encapsulate me. To get a taste of the wine on his lips and…

Okay, Maggie. That's enough. It's only been a year.

A year. Even Caitlyn said that was long enough. She said she was sorry and she apologized to Grayson too, and that's about as much blessing as I'm going to get from her.

But I don't want to tell Josie yet that I want to kiss Grayson. Because what if it doesn't happen? It's too much pressure, so I text something else instead.

Maggie: I don't know yet. I'll come up with something. Any ideas?

Josie: I think your ideas are going to be a whole lot better than mine.

Josie: But whatever it is you think up, I'm sure he's going to love it. Have fun.

After pulling a sweater on over my tank top, I say a quick goodbye to Jovi before heading out of the house and down the grassy knoll toward the dunes. The night has suddenly cleared from the Eastern Port rain, leaving a coolness in the air that wasn't there before. Though there are clouds, a multitude of stars can be seen hanging bright in the sky, little pinpricks of ivory light poking through a dark blanket. And better yet, the moon is bright and reflects off the water, a haze sitting over the ocean near the shore, the fog thickening as I head down toward the sea's edge, eventually engulfing me.

The shopping bag's contents bang against me as I hoist it up over my arm in order to climb the dune. I kick off my shoes and place them in the bag as well, realizing that I've forgotten to bring glasses for Grayson and me to drink from. I could run back to the house. There might be enough time, but I don't want to risk not having everything set up when he arrives. It's very adult to drink white wine out of a shared bottle, right? Thinking of the bottle, I never checked if it's a twist-off cap or one that has a cork, and I didn't bring a corkscrew. Maybe Grayson will know how to smash the top off, like they do when christening a new ship.

I tell myself that it's fine—and everything *will* be fine—the whole climb up the sandy hill. As I slip-slide down the other side in the dark and mist, I have to steady myself from being knocked off-kilter with my bag. When I get over the boulders and land onto the sandy beach, the area is expectedly empty, and the lapping of the midnight blue waves is like gentle and soothing music to my ears.

I don't venture too far from the entrance before I find the perfect spot. The StopShop Grocery Mart bag crinkles as I set it in the sand, and I quickly begin pulling out its contents. Placing the blanket down, I weigh the corners against the breeze with the solar lights. They're already bright and glistening with an egg-yolk-colored glow when I remove them from between the other items. The candles get shoved somewhat lovingly in the sand and lit with the barbecue torch, while the wine—complete with a twist-off cap, thankfully—finds a home in the center of the blanket, perched precariously among the bumps in the shore.

Standing back toward the boulders, I admire my haphazard handiwork. Small flames flicker from the candles between the spot where I've laid the blanket and the calm ripples of the ocean. They cast a similar color to the lanterns but not as much light, the fleur-de-lis patterns on the iron edges of the solar lights making skewed shapes on the fabric and off the glass of the wine bottle. It's pretty and serene and dreamy... at least to me.

I'm so caught up that I almost don't hear the footsteps coming down over the dunes, the sound of someone sliding over the boulders behind me nearly lost in the flow of the waves. It's the voice that catches my breath first, low and deep and gentle, letting me know right away that I've done something right.

"Wow, Maggie."

I turn slowly to face Grayson, who is standing there in the glimmer of the lights and the moon in a dark, tight shirt, a light hoodie, and a pair of khaki shorts, his sneakers in one hand. The ripple of his muscles against his clothes is only accentuated in the evening light. For a moment, I allow myself to look at him because I think he's letting himself look at me too. I can almost pick out the clear blue of his eyes despite the darkness, and the way they look in the flickering candlelight says more to me than any words ever could.

But even still, I ask. "Do you like it?"

A smile quirks up at the corners of his lips, small at first, but then bigger and brighter. "Of course I like it. It's beautiful. Perfect weather, nice lighting, and you even brought some wine. Very romantic."

"I forgot the glasses and a bottle opener." I shrug. "But I did happen to bring wine with a twist-off cap, so thank goodness for small miracles."

Grayson chuckles, reaching for my hand and taking my fingers in between his. They're warm and soft, and feeling his touch makes me warm and soft on the inside too. "Should we open it up then? Or did you want to go for a little walk first?"

"Do you think anyone will take our things if we leave them here?" I gesture with my free hand around the deserted beach with a small laugh, Grayson joining in before we head toward the water's edge and saunter aimlessly underneath the moon and stars.

The night is quiet, no evening birds calling, no sound from the dockyard. There's just the noise of us together, our feet on the sand, the sea at our toes, and the beating of our hearts. We don't say anything for a while, comfortable in our own silence, until Grayson delicately tugs me to a stop and stares up at the moon. I look as well, scanning for divots in its surface that might be visible with the naked eye while wondering what he sees up there.

"My mother used to tell me a story about the moon," he begins, his tone soft. "That if you look up at it when you're with someone, I mean really stop and look up at it, and they look up too, for a moment you're both able to connect. A deep connection, like an invisible string between yourself and them. A tide of hearts."

The words resonate with me immediately, reminding me of the barbecue only a few nights before when I considered the way that Grayson and I were touching, the little space between our knees like strings—even when you pull them apart, there's still something there, a reminder of the other person that lasts even after you've separated. I never used the words "invisible string" out loud, but it's funny in a coincidental sort of way.

"What does that mean, then, that I looked up at the moon with you?" I break my gaze from the sky and look over at Grayson, who smiles but still looks up.

"Maybe it means nothing. Maybe it means that just there, for a second, we were given the opportunity for something more than what we had before this moment."

"That's beautiful when you put it that way. I've never thought about the moon as offering a connection between two people."

"Honestly, Maggie, I never really did either until now. But I think I just figured out what she meant."

With a small grin, I don't hesitate to look back up at the sky, no longer searching for craters. Instead, I'm thinking about how if Taylor's soul is made of the stars of the night sky, Grayson's heart can be connected to the moon. Maybe all the special people in our lives are connected to us through nature and the sky and the earth: the ocean, the celestial bodies, the grassy knoll behind one's house that leads to memories both new and old.

After a few minutes tick by, Grayson peeks over at me. "Want to head toward the dockyard a bit before we turn around?"

"Sure. Nice night for a walk since the heat broke with the rain."

He squeezes my hand and we make our way down the beach, stopping every so often along the shoreline, the fringes of the water tickling our toes and making our feet damp as we playfully kick water at each other like children. Grayson manages to spot a piece of beach glass in the dark, the sparkling blue catching a glint of moonlight. He picks it up and hands it to me like he knows it will be something that I'll want. He isn't wrong. So many good things in my memories are blue, like his eyes.

"The color reminds me of that wall in your house. The new one you painted." Grayson grins. "Did you ever get that painting up?"

I shake my head as I run a finger along the smooth edges of the worn glass before putting it in my shorts pocket. "I didn't. Not yet. I didn't have time after I got off the phone with you. But I will."

"That's good. I think it'll suit the space there. I have to admit, it'll be kind of neat to come over some time and see one of my photographs as a painting on your wall."

"Sometimes I get pictures of my commissions hanging on people's walls. It's a great feeling. Makes the work worth it, especially if I've been feeling uninspired."

"Do you still feel that way?"

"No." I shake my head with a smile. "I still have six more of your photographs to paint sitting in my inbox. I don't think I'll be uninspired for a long time."

"You're going to paint them all?"

"Why not? I don't have any more commissions after I finish the project for Darlene Cross. It's about time I do a little painting for myself."

He slides a hand along my arm; I can't feel the warmth through the sleeve of my sweater, but his touch makes me tingly down through my legs to my toes. "I'm so happy to hear that, Maggie. I'm glad I could help."

Little does he know that he's been able to help me more than I could ever put into words.

"Come on." I tug at his hand. "Let's see if our wine is still there. I think we both deserve something to drink after all this walking."

"I'll race you back to the blanket?"

"What are we, in high school?" I laugh, but the laughter is buried by Grayson taking off into the dark, kicking up sand like Jovi and Perdita do when they play on the beach. I let out an amused snort to myself, but then I break into a run as well, heart beating in time with the slamming of my feet into the sand, and for a minute, I am free—free of thoughts and worry and apprehension. And then I know what my surprise is going to be. I'm definitely going to kiss Grayson tonight.

We make it back to the blanket in record time, the candles still lit despite the rising breeze. Grayson beats me by at least a minute, and he's pretending to stare down at his watch when I approach as if to jokingly tell me that he's been waiting for me forever.

"Hey, you're supposed to be in good shape if you're in the military." I try and catch my breath. "I'm just a reclusive painter who walks her dog."

As I brush sand from my feet and take a seat on the knitted throw, Grayson reaches over and uncaps the wine bottle. The seal makes a noise as it breaks, and then he hands the drink to me so I can have the first sip.

I take the bottle from his hand, its rounded body covered in slippery condensation. My wedding ring clinks on the side. "You sure you don't mind sharing my germs?"

"I think I like your germs, Maggie."

The words make me blush, but thanks to the darkness, I don't think Grayson can see. As a distraction, I tip the bottle to my mouth and take a gulp of the white wine, the taste of alcohol and peaches and some kind of fragrant flower running over my tongue and down the back of my throat. It's refreshing after the unexpected run along the beach.

I give the bottle back to Grayson and he takes a small sip. Clearing his throat, he asks, "Did you ever think that we'd be here?"

"No. I never thought that I'd be here with anyone ever again after Taylor. I fell into my own routine and sadness. I thought that was just what life was going to be like from then on, you know?"

He takes another drink, the liquid sloshing inside the glass bottle before he hands it over to me. "I understand. I mean, I don't really, but I can imagine it must feel horrible to lose a partner like that. When I delivered that letter, I had no idea what was inside. I didn't think I'd ever see you again. I didn't think much of anything, really. I was just taking Perdi for a walk and figured I'd make the delivery at the same time."

I take two drinks from the wine and look into the distance, way out where the dark blue of the water meets the deep black of the sky. "It's funny how things work out sometimes."

Grayson's just about to open his mouth to say something when, without warning, the sky opens up, sheets of rain pouring down on us. We're soaked as instantly as it starts, the candles fizzling out and their jars filling with small puddles of water, our clothes drenched from our unsheltered spot underneath the moon. We don't have enough time to get to Grayson's car or under one of the rocky overhangs farther down the beach; there's no time for anything because we are soaked, the blanket is soaked, and our hair sticks to our faces.

Then I laugh, Grayson laughs, and we're looking at the wine, each other, and up at the night with open hands like we're going to gather the water falling from the sky above. It's the second—or maybe third—time that our eyes meet that I recognize a softness in Grayson's gaze, similar to the night I spent at his house before I told him that I hadn't been alone in a bedroom without Jovi since Taylor passed. It's a gentle look, a thoughtful one, but there's a little fire burning brightly behind those blue eyes, and I know it's the perfect chance for my surprise.

Before I give myself time to hesitate, I lean over on the soaked throw blanket and Grayson dips toward me. With the hand that's not holding the wine bottle, he brushes sopping hair from my cheek with grace.

"Maggie?"

The way he says my name hitches my breath in my throat, and for a moment, between the rain and his voice, I think I'm drowning. But despite this, I take my hand and wrap it behind his neck, burying my fingers in his shirt. The scent of vanilla permeates the air as I get closer, mixed with ocean salt and wet seagrass.

"Grayson." His name isn't a question when it leaves my lips, not as it might once have been. Instead, it feels like the first stroke of paint on a fresh white canvas, filled with opportunity for whatever is to come.

We're close now, so close that I can practically taste the mint toothpaste on his breath, combined with the sweet scent of white wine. It's intoxicating on its own, and my fingers twitch, sinking him into my touch as I close my eyes and gently press my lips to his.

For a moment, there's the rain around us—dripping onto our soaked clothes and running rivers off our saturated hair. But that awareness only lasts a split second before there's nothing more in the world except for the two of us. We're kissing there next to the sandy dunes, the storm-colored boulders, and the great wide ocean that seems to be a different hue every time I look at it. Even though my eyes are closed, I see a thousand shades of black and blue and sparkles of gray behind my eyelids. But more than that, more than anything, I *feel*.

Grayson's hand finds my cheek and I pull him in closer as the rain continues to pour, my heart smashing against my ribs and my toes tingling. He deepens the kiss and I can't help the little sigh that escapes me, and with that sigh comes a small groan from him where we dance with our tongues and paint pictures of this moment in our memories.

What was once a shattered yellow glow coming through a window in my mind suddenly becomes mixed with a shade of blue. The two blend together in my mind like an ocean and a sandy seashore, rising and falling with the tides in a gentle watercolor that I'll never be able to replicate. And that's okay. Because sometimes the colors in our minds are the most beautiful. Colors painted by grief and love and loss and moving on make each of us into a painting of our own.

We gently break from our kiss, the rain hammering down on our bodies, soaking the blanket and the beach. And until the rain dissipates into a quiet drizzle, we sit there and stare up at the moon. The downpour doesn't matter. We're already wet and we're together and I recognize that my grief boat is still floating. I'm still above the theoretical water of the fictional grief ocean described by the resource therapist. I'm—*dare I think it?*—moving forward.

As I'm looking upward, a flash catches my eye right next to the milky white of the moon. Tingles find their way from my brain down my spine, and I'm immediately reminded of Taylor's letter.

Maybe consider this: when you wish on stars from now on or see the rain or watch out the window for a ship to come into the dockyard, know I'm a little piece of you as well.

"Did you see that?" I point into the darkness. Squinting, I try my hardest to see if maybe there are more shooting stars, but that seems to have been the only one.

Grayson shakes his head, brushing a trickle of rain from his jaw. "What was it?"

Smiling to myself, I reach across his lap for the wine bottle and take another cool drink. Perhaps it was a figment of my imagination, or maybe I've just been hoping for a sign from above. Either way, I've received what's probably my final message from Taylor in the stars tonight. And it was everything I could have wanted.

"Never mind," I reply, leaning back against Grayson's shoulder. "It was nothing."

Chapter Seventeen

The rain passes as quickly as it came, our clothes never quite drying. Grayson and I finish off the bottle of wine, passing it back and forth, sitting there on the wet blanket. We talk for so long that we almost don't notice the chill in the air. I'm not sure what time it is when I start to shiver—I've left my phone on the kitchen island—but Grayson notices and pulls his device from his pocket before announcing that it's midnight. Strokes of bold blackish-blue and distant city lights glimmer on the horizon, while the minor effects of the peach-flavored wine combined with the kiss bubble in my veins, only to settle in that soft spot in the back of my neck where I get the electric feeling every time that he touches me.

Stifling a yawn, I lean against Grayson's damp shoulder for some body heat and think about what's going to happen next. I don't want to leave the beach, but I forgot to let Jovi out before coming down, and goosebumps are rising on my arms and legs from the mixture of rain and the salty breeze.

"Do you want to come up to the house?" I whisper, switching my gaze from the rolling-in clouds to Grayson's hands on my knee. There's no invisible string there anymore, no emptiness between us. We're touching, we've touched, and this is real.

He nods, squeezing my leg gently. "Sure. It's getting a little cold. Especially since we're still wet. I think I have some dry clothes in the car, and while I'm up there, I can help you hang that painting… if you still want to put it up."

"I do."

Grayson and I gather the items I brought down to the beach: the candles, the solar lanterns, the blanket, the barbecue lighter, and the wine bottle. It all gets shoved back in the StopShop Grocery Mart bag that's somehow almost completely dry, and Grayson heaves it over his shoulder before gesturing for me to head up the rocks. Grabbing my soaked shoes, I clamber over the weather-beaten boulders before trekking over the dunes, stopping at the very top to make sure that Grayson's followed. When he catches up, I step and slide down the seagrass-lined pathway, landing next to his hatchback parked on the side of the street.

He sets the bag down on the sandy roadside, slipping on his sneakers before fetching his car keys from his pocket. They jingle in the quiet of the night as he pops open the car's hatch to expose a well-organized trunk: a flat of water bottles, some dog toys in a plastic bin, and a backpack filled with what I can only assume are supplies and dry clothes.

"You're more prepared than I expected." I laugh a little because that's what I said to him when he had me over the night of the barbecue.

Amusingly enough, he replies with the same answer he gave me that time as well. "I'm in the military. It's part of my job to be prepared."

Unzipping the bag, he rummages around for a second before tugging out a pair of rolled-up jeans and a gray T-shirt. He unrolls the clothes and places them over his shoulder before closing the bag and then the trunk. I don't know why I watch him do all of this; it's like I can't take my eyes off him since we kissed, and every inch of me wants to kiss him again, here next to the car, in the dark, while the rest of Eastern Port is probably sleeping. When Grayson hoists the crinkling bag back up onto his shoulder, the sound drops me back from my imagination to the side of the road, and I uncerimoniously slip on my shoes. They immediately get filled with grains of sand.

"Do you want to bring the car up to the house?" I straighten again, shuffling my feet inside my shoes to try and shift the granules into a more comfortable position.

Grayson shakes his head. "It's okay. I don't mind walking back down the hill."

"Okay."

We head across the empty road, no sign of any cars all the way down the shoreline, before traipsing through the backyard and approaching the house. Little white moths dance around the porch light, their wings flicking against the small glass panels, while Jovi's nose pokes against the window to the side of the door, smudging the glass. His pile of driftwood sits, unmoved, along the porch railing, the paint just starting to peel on the boards around it. It takes Jovi a second to realize that it's me coming home, and when he does, he backs away from the entrance and lets out a single bark.

I open the door and Jovi wags his fluffy tail, prancing around Grayson and me as we try to squeeze through. He's excited to see Grayson more than he is to see me. Even despite his happiness at the visitor, when I shoo him out of the house into the yard, he only pauses for a second to let Grayson give him a scratch behind the ears, and then he careens out of the house in all his puppy glory. This gives us room to breathe, to close the door, kick off our shoes, and for Grayson to place the bag down on the floor next to the dining room table.

"If you want to get changed into your dry clothes, the bathroom is down the hall on the right. Head toward the studio." I can't remember if I gave him a full tour of the house when he was over the first night. The whole evening was kind of a blur—it still is. Then again, I think tonight will be a blur, but in a different way.

Grayson nods and walks down the hall as I tug off my sweatshirt and hang it on the rack by the door to dry. Even my white shirt underneath is wet, and my shorts are sticking to my legs uncomfortably, now that I'm acutely aware of them. I rush into the bedroom and dig out a pair of black leggings and a soft pink long-sleeved shirt, changing into them and re-knotting my hair in a bun before heading into the studio and flicking on the light.

The studio's glow is almost too bright, and it doesn't match the mood of the evening. This evening has been soft and gentle and emotional, even including the torrential downpour. As I look at the completed canvas in the corner of the room, it's a bit funny because though the painting is moody and gray, it somehow fits. Maybe it's because it's from Grayson's photograph and I feel more connected to him now. Perhaps it has something to do with having finished the letter from Taylor. It's possible that it also reflects on my grief ship, the boat I've been living on for the last year, the one that nearly capsized with every change, every passing minute, and every memory.

I run my finger along one edge of the artwork, feeling the bumps of thicker paint on the painted waves. It's all dry now, hardened on the canvas after many hours, and the texture of the piece makes it feel like I'm back on the beach that day when Jovi wound his leash around Grayson and me and we first bumped together. My wedding band glints off the incandescence, and I bite the inside of my lip.

The brightness is still too harsh in here, so I swap the overhead lighting for the lamp on the small table next to my computer desk and printer.

Much better.

A floorboard creaks as Grayson crosses the room, and I turn. He's wearing his dry clothes, his blond hair still damp and shoved over to one side, while his cheeks are a deep pink from the chill of the outdoors. "That looks amazing, Maggie."

"It only turned out because of your photography skills."

Grayson shakes his head, standing slightly behind me as we both look at the art. "I disagree. I think your painting skills had a lot to do with it. I mean, here." He points to the waves I was running my finger along only a minute before. "The way you've captured the water is stunning. I remember reading somewhere that water and fire are some of the hardest things to capture in art. I think you've done it though."

I peer at him over my shoulder and he's closer than I expected. I register the scent of vanilla and rain first, then the feeling of his body near mine. Letting out a little chuckle, I can't help but ask, "Since when are you an art connoisseur?"

Grayson's hand finds mine, and he gently spins me to face him, the lamplight glistening in his blue eyes. The blue that caused me to rush to House 'N Home for "sea breeze" paint. The blue that helped me cover my Taylor yellow wall in the living room. The blue that I thought about for some time before I even knew the color would mean something to me. I melt into the touch, into the sensation of his rough, but also somehow soft, fingers. I could kiss him right now, I really could, but I want another perfect moment, another rainstorm.

"Maybe I just want to be a Maggie connoisseur." A smile twinges at the corners of my lips, and soon he grins as well. "But maybe we can start with getting this painting on the wall. I also happened to read somewhere that you can tell a lot about a person by how they hang a picture."

I scrunch my face. "How do you find time to read all these random things?"

Grayson shrugs, delicately dropping my hand and taking a step toward the large painting. "Night watch."

Fifteen minutes later, I've certainly learned a few things just by watching Grayson hang the painting on the "sea breeze" wall in the living room. First, that he has a great eye for finding the center of a room without having to pull out a measuring tape; second, that his shoulder muscles ripple with every movement of the hammer in his hand; and third, that even though I live next to the part of the ocean depicted in the artwork, I swear I hear the sound of the waves when I stand next to the canvas to check out his handiwork. It's kind of like when children hold up conch shells to their ears and are told they can hear the sea inside, only I'm in my living room next to a man I'm absolutely falling for, smelling vanilla and musk.

"What do you think?" Grayson's in the middle of the living room, watching every one of my movements with a careful gaze until I go and stand next to him.

"It's perfect. You were right. I love it in here."

He beams, a smile crossing his face from cheek to cheek. "I'm so glad to hear that. Maybe you can paint some of the other ones on smaller canvases and make a collage. An ocean accent wall."

"That's not a bad idea. Especially since I feel like I'm going to have a hard time wanting to sell anything made from a photograph you took."

Grayson runs a hand over his hair. "Why's that? Isn't selling paintings your job?"

"I guess I've fallen for the pictures. They remind me…" I hesitate, trying to decide who they remind me of more, Taylor or Grayson. But as I think, I realize that it's more the latter than the former. I have so many memories to remind me of Taylor, even though I've broken his "you're egg-cellent" mug and donated his clothes and finally used up all that orange mint toothpaste he liked to hoard. Those memories, the stories, that mess in my head are still there, and they're mine.

"Everything okay?"

I look up from the floor where my gaze has fallen, giving Grayson a quick once over. He's standing there with a hammer in his hand, nails in his jeans pocket, and a dark gray shirt stretched across his shoulders. And, as I allow my glance to drift over him, I also acknowledge that I have emotions and needs and wants and desires that extend past my grief. That my grief boat is no longer a life raft, but maybe has floated ashore. That I'm somewhere new, and even though I'm leaving the boat behind and it's a bit scary, I have someone to go on my next adventure with, even if it does involve said person going out to sea and leaving me behind every once in a while. Perhaps, more than anything else, I don't feel guilty anymore.

"Maggie?" Grayson tilts his head to the side, a little like Jovi does, which reminds me that the dog is still outside in the yard.

As if he knows I'm thinking about him, Jovi bursts through the slightly ajar front door, a rocket of puppy energy and gray fluff. Zooming around the living room, bouncing from couch to chair and back again, Grayson and I watch and laugh as Jovi locates his stuffed squeaky pig buried under a cushion, then tosses it up in the air before catching it in his mouth. That amuses him for only a couple of seconds before he bounds toward me at full speed, jumping against me with his front paws for attention. I'm barely able to keep him from knocking me over, and I step and twist around to catch myself, saved once again by Grayson's quick reach and almost instant reaction.

It's in that moment that everything comes full circle, and I have a flashback to the beach where Jovi and Perdi tangled Grayson and me up for the first time. We've been tangled up so many times figuratively since that encounter. Tangled with leashes and invisible strings, tangled with emotions and feelings and other people's arguments. Tangled with grief and the past and what could be for the future.

Grayson holds me by the arms, hammer still in one hand and pressing against my sleeve, waiting for me to regain my balance. My hands are on his chest and I can feel the heavy beating of his heart under my palms, and it makes my own quicken. I bite my bottom lip and allow myself to freely melt into the fireworks feeling that's spreading along my skin from where he's touching me. Slipping my touch up to his shoulders, then behind his neck, as Jovi barks and bounces around our legs, I bump us as close together as we could possibly be.

I want to kiss Grayson again. I want to kiss him without inhibition, without having to stop for the downpour or the time. And maybe I don't need another perfect moment, another rainstorm, another second where I know if I wait to have him, my whole body might burn. Because my heart is on fire right now, my skin is electric, and I've finally pieced together a million pieces of my broken soul. Right here in the living room, hammer in hand, Jovi barking in the background, is enough. It will always be enough with Grayson.

So, I stand up on my tiptoes, stretching as high as I can get, and Grayson dips down in one smooth movement to meet me. The hammer seemingly disappears into a void, because a moment later, both of Grayson's hands are soft on my hips, before lifting me into the air, and pulling me into his hard body. I wrap my legs around his narrow waist, crossing my ankles together behind his back to secure myself as he slips his hands along my spine, giving me shivers from my toes up to the top of my head. My fingers find the neckline of his shirt, my mind remembering the scar that's hidden underneath, and, unable to wait any longer, I wrap the fabric around my hands and pull him into my lips.

The kiss sends sparks off inside of me, deep and heavy ones that are a rainstorm of their own. They settle in the pit of my stomach and keep me wanting more. And Grayson gives. And I give back. We consume one another's passion until Jovi stops barking and our lips are chapped. And even then, we don't stop. We take a moment to breathe, to touch, to measure our existence outside of one another, but we don't stop, not for a long while.

Later, much later, we make it to the couch, curled up in one another's arms like we were in Grayson's bed after the barbecue. Jovi's on the chair, asleep and snoring, and I'm staring with my eyes half-shut at the "sea breeze" wall and my new artwork as Grayson absently twirls his finger over my exposed side.

As I lay there, I adjust my left arm from under me, exposing the gold wedding band on my finger. I watch the way the cuts in the metal twinkle against the kitchen light in the background, a small diamond at the top reflecting the dim glow. I could probably remove the ring now. After all, it's been a year.

Then, out of the corner of my eye, I see it. A little patch of yellow in the top corner of the blue wall, probably covered by haphazardly placed painter's tape. It's like a bit of Taylor peeking in, saying hello, reminding me to love myself and let him go—like a tiny egg yolk star at the edge of a sea of Caribbean blue.

Fine print used to be on one of my paint tubes that called the shade "lemon balm" which I hated, because the word "balm" is too close to "bomb," and the thought of anything crashing and burning was too close to my memories of last summer. I just called the paint "egg yolk" for a long time, which I dislike slightly less until now. I used to say that it was because at least eggs had happy memories: Taylor making me breakfast in bed on the weekends, his last birthday cake that I tried to bake, that time we vacationed at a farm in Charlottetown and were able to pick out our own eggs for brunch.

But now, I call the shade what it is. It's lemon balm. Because "balm" doesn't have to mean "bomb," just like some things mean more than you'd ever expect. Yellow, blue, the moon, the stars, a lost love letter delivered by someone you'd otherwise never have met.

Gently, with my other hand, I twist the ring off and place it on the coffee table.

"What're you doing?" Grayson asks, the words murmured together.

I bring my hand back, rubbing the empty space on my finger with my thumb. There's an indent there, a subtle one, but I can feel it—it's smoother than the rest of the skin. I think about slipping the ring back on, just in case that indent ever goes away. But it doesn't matter if it does. Just because things disappear doesn't mean they weren't valued or important. Just because Taylor's gone, it doesn't signify that I loved him any less.

"Maggie?" Grayson shifts, leaning up and over my shoulder. I tilt my head back and stare deep into his 'sea breeze' blue eyes with a weight lifted off my chest.

Smiling, I run my now-naked hand across his stubbled cheek. "Nothing much. Just letting go."

Acknowledgments

THANK YOU FOR LOVING ME was a project that felt like it would never end. I mean that in both a good way and a bad one, depending on what day of the week I happen to be referring to, and what month of the year I made the attempt to work on the story. I often feel like so many books (along with their acknowledgments) focus on the wonderful parts of the world. However, with this story, even though it's a book about hope and learning to move forward, is truly a narrative about grief and the ways in which it can affect someone. Because of this focus, I'm almost strangely thankful for the never ending-ness of the drafting and editing process because it has made this book all the more real in my experience.

This story would never have come to be without the help of so many people, from my husband, Jesse to Lara and Bri, Zilla, Kristin, so many of my Discord and Wattpad friends, the amazing people at Midnight Tide Publishing and Silver Shell Publishing, and my always-wonderful editor, Jennia. There are so many people who gave me thoughts, read over pieces of the story, asked questions, gave examples, and who offered little bits of connection with the plot that I'm certain I'm missing some people.

However, thank you so much for everything you've ever done for this project. It truly has been a joy.

Lastly, please know that if you are on a grief ship, there are resources that are available to help you.

MyGrief.ca by Canadian Virtual Hospice
mygrief.ca

Canadian Mental Health Association – Grieving
cmha.ca/brochure/grieving/

The Dougy Center: The National Center for Grieving Children & Families
dougy.org

About the Author

NICOLE BEA writes deep stories to dig into: atmospheric women's fiction and upper young adult novels with themes of self-discovery through the power of love. By daylight, she works as a technical writer and project manager for an international medical company, while by starlight, she pens all the stories taking up space in her head.

Nicole and her husband share their home in Eastern Canada with a collection of multi-colored cats, a cupboard stuffed with tea, and a lifetime's worth of books.

Find her online at:

https://campsite.bio/nicbeawrites
https://instagram.com/nicbeawrites

Also By Nicole Bea

The Things We Couldn't Save

Clarke and Katie have been best friends since elementary school, sharing sleepovers, pizza bagel recipes, and their jobs at a failing ice cream shop. But Katie's new relationship with Nick, a street racer from a rival high school, leaves Clarke behind. She fills the Katie-shaped hole in her life with Nick's best friend and fellow racer, Zayne.

But this is not a love story.

As Clarke and Zayne fall for one another, Clarke's world is rocked with the thrill of street racing, binge drinking, and living in a moment where it feels like everything is changing. In her rush to become the version of herself Zayne says he loves, Clarke starts to lose touch with the person she is. Soon, Clarke's transformation into a girl who lives on the edge becomes an ultimatum: what is she willing to leave behind when summer ends?

Manufactured by Amazon.ca
Bolton, ON